PERFECTLY IMPERFECT
Ruby Yayra Goka

TECHMATE PUBLISHERS LTD
2014

First published in Ghana in 2014 by Techmate Publishers Ltd.
P. O. Box 6667, Accra North, Ghana.
techmatepublisher@gmail.com

Cover image by Jennifer Jacobs

ISBN 978-9988-1949-56

The Burt Award for African Literature recognises excellence in young adult fiction from African countries. It supports the writing and publication of high quality, culturally relevant books and ensures their distribution to schools and libraries to help develop young people's literacy skills and foster their love of reading. The Burt Award is generously sponsored by the Canadian philanthropist, Bill Burt, and is part of the ongoing literacy programmes of the Ghana Book Trust and of CODE, a Canadian NGO which has been supporting development through education for over 50 years.

For my nieces:

Anne Goka
Rita Goka
Paula Sallah
Yaayaa Sallah
Maya Logo

And also for:

Yayra Dotse
Dorcas Yayra Ahiable
Blessing Uche

Being happy doesn't mean that everything is perfect. It means you've decided to look beyond the imperfections.

Anonymous

C h a p t e r

1

I killed my father.

Each morning that's the first thought that jumps into my head. It's also the last thought I have at night before I sleep. I know my mother blames me but she's never said so. I've caught her staring at me a number of times. Each time I pretend that I don't know she's staring. Once I turned to look at her and she turned away quickly. We never speak about it. We never mention my father anymore. We just pretend that it never happened.

It's another morning, another day. I killed my father. I'm the reason he died.

*

"And one! . . . And two! . . . And three! . . . That's it! You're doing just fine. Feel those muscles shaping up. That's it . . . Good job!"

I rolled over in my bed and buried my head under my pillow. The fitness instructor from Mama's 'Walk Your Way to a

Healthier, Fitter You' DVD kept her pieces of encouragement coming. I could picture the woman with a wide smile on her made-up face on the TV screen. She would be in a tank top and sweat shorts, her pony tail bouncing behind her as she barely broke into a sweat.

I could also imagine my mother. She would be standing in front of the TV in an old T-shirt, a hair net and jogging pants, huffing and puffing with every breath as she followed the steps. Her shirt would be stuck to her body; sweat would be pouring down her face, her back and her arms. The look on her face would be one of sheer torture. She'd grunt and groan through the entire thirty minutes of the work-out and then collapse in a heap on the floor where she'd stay for five minutes muttering, "Enough! Enough of this! I can't do this anymore" before she'd head for the shower and get ready for her day. But I knew better. At exactly 5:30 a.m. tomorrow, she'd be in front of the TV going through this same routine. My mother believes in plans and routines. Aerobic exercise is part of my mother's routine. A routine she never departs from, come rain, sunshine, harmattan or even the death of her husband.

My father died nine months ago. We were in a car accident together. He died. I survived. His life stopped. My life is on hold. My mother's life continued the same as ever. As if nothing happened. I'm 99.99% sure that the day after the accident she woke up at 5:20 a.m. and ten minutes later, she was in front of the TV doing her aerobics. The 0.01% doubt arises because I wasn't home so I can't say for sure whether she did continue with her exercises or not. I spent the first three months in a hospital and most of the other six undergoing physiotherapy. I had broken a bone in my left leg, two ribs and dislocated a shoulder. I also had a broken nose, broken cheek bones, a fractured eye socket, a compound fracture of my right hand (that means the bone broke and stuck out of my skin). My back and left arm are a criss-cross of scar tissue. I needed eighty-two stitches on my face alone. The left side of my face is dead and I'm not just talking of the ugly scars. I have three of them—one over my eyebrow to my ear, the second from the bridge of my nose to the corner of my lip and the third, which doesn't show so much, at the angle of my jaw—I'm talking dead where I can't feel anything. The doctors said it was nerve damage and are hopeful sensation will return in time. I'm not so optimistic.

People call me lucky. I call them ignorant. I am a lot of things but lucky isn't one of them. What sort of luck makes you kill your own dad? When people stare at my scars I know they're wondering—*what could have happened to her?* Most times I just look away. I don't bother answering their unasked questions. The scars are my punishment. They are the cross I have to bear. I'm like Cain in the Bible who got a mark put on his face so that anywhere he went people would know he killed his brother.

*

I drifted back to sleep and woke up when the sun was high up in the sky. I could hear the movers. Mama was instructing them on what to do. I knew they'd have to come and get my stuff too. I got off the mattress. The bed had already been dismantled and the separate pieces were stacked by the wall. I brushed my teeth without looking in the mirror, I was becoming very good at that. I took a quick shower and had just finished attaching the colostomy bag when I heard Mama at the door. I've had the bag since I was thirteen.

When I was twelve I was diagnosed with inflammatory bowel disease which meant I had very bad abdominal pain, passed mostly bloody stool and had to use the toilet a lot more times than the average person. 'A lot more' means the disease sent me running to the toilet about fifteen to twenty times a day. If I wasn't fast enough I ended up soiling myself like a baby. I always took two extra sets of uniforms to school just in case I soiled myself. I got laughed at a lot and I didn't have any friends. It was much worse at night. There's no way you can get a good night's sleep if you have to wake up every thirty minutes to pass stool. It was distressing not just for me but for my parents too. Once I bled so much that I required a blood transfusion and had to stay in the hospital for three weeks. That was when Mama insisted I had surgery to remove my large intestines and part of my rectum. That also meant I needed to get a temporary colostomy.

After I'd had the colostomy done, my parents moved me to the elite private SHS where my father taught mathematics. I think it was a sort of bribe for what they had been forced to do to me. Of course it didn't hurt either that my two best friends,

Sofi and Dede attended the same school. The fact that no one in Higher Heights knew about the disease helped a lot. I could pretend to be normal.

I can now talk about the colostomy like it wasn't a big deal but it was. Even though I used to get very severe diarrhoea, was sick most of the time and had to miss school a lot, I couldn't imagine having to defecate through a hole in my abdomen. My colostomy means that I defecate through my abdomen. I hated it. I hated the very thought of it. I hated my mother for insisting that that was the best thing for me to do.

After the surgery I wouldn't even look at the stoma, the opening through which the faeces come out. I wouldn't look at it. I wouldn't change the bag. I wouldn't do anything. I figured that since Mama was so insistent on me having the surgery done she could do the honours. She did. For three months after my operation, Mama changed the bags and kept my stoma clean. I did not lift a finger to help her. All I did was worry about how my best friends, Dede and Sofi, would react to the stoma. The first time I told them they didn't freak out or anything. Dede even wanted to touch it so I let her. It didn't hurt. It never hurts. The doctors say it has no nerve endings so I can't feel pain. Knowing that Dede and Sofi were cool about it, I began to take care of it myself. I didn't tell anyone else, though. Now it's got to the point where I don't think about it at all, I mean it's just like another part of my body, like my nose or ears or belly-button. And who spends their time worrying about their nose or ears or belly-buttons?

*

"Good morning, sleep well?" Mama was on her knees, taping a box closed.

I mumbled a reply and headed downstairs to the kitchen. She had bought me *waakye*, with all the trimmings, even two pieces of *wele*. I appreciated the gesture but I wished she wouldn't try so hard to pretend we were okay, to pretend that life was perfect, to pretend that a third person was not missing from our midst. She followed me into the kitchen and made a half-hearted attempt to get me excited about the move, but I ignored her. She settled for watching me eat instead, like she had never seen food enter a person's mouth and disappear down their throat.

"I wish we didn't have to move too."

"Then tell them to stop. Tell them to put our things back." I nearly choked on my food. I was afraid that I was going to cry.

"We can't stay here anymore. The lease is almost up and I honestly can't afford to pay for another three years. Besides, this is a great opportunity for us."

A great opportunity for you. We've had this conversation a thousand times already. Nothing I said now was going to make her change her mind.

"It's a great opportunity for you too," Mama said as if she could read my thoughts. "You'll meet new people, make new friends. It's a fresh start for both of us. Please try and be happy about it."

"Madam, ah beg, come see somtin," one of the workers

called from the doorway. Mama got up and followed him out.

Mama *claimed* we were broke. It had been Daddy who had taken care of our finances. She said somehow their savings had disappeared out of their joint bank account. There wasn't any money to renew the lease on the house or to pay fees for the private school I attended. I knew she was lying and I hated her for it. Blame the dead guy who wasn't there to defend himself. The *only* reason we were moving was because *she* had finally got the job of her dreams. She was going to become the medical superintendent of the district hospital in Sogakofe. The fact that she was the first female to hold that position only added to the allure of the job.

She had always wanted to be in an upper management position. It was why she had taken long-distance courses and used her annual leave for sandwich programmes.

She was so excited about the job offer I couldn't believe she was the same woman who had buried her husband less than a year ago. How do you bounce right back into life without mourning a man you spent twenty years of your life with?

Apart from the step up in salary, the other benefits that came with the job were—a three bedroom bungalow; water, electricity and phone bills paid by the hospital; and a monthly allowance that was almost half her current salary.

She didn't care that I knew no one in Sogakofe or that it was hard enough that people in a neighbourhood I had spent all my life in still stared at my face and my left hand and whispered all sorts of things behind my back. What would people I didn't know do? She didn't care that I'd have to repeat a class and be in a class full of juniors I didn't even know. She cared only about her stupid job and making more money.

*

I was still eating, when my two best friends, Dede Odartey and Sophia Asare, walked into the kitchen. Dede was in jeans, a tie-and-dye T-shirt and black ballet flats. I know that even if I live to be a hundred, I'll never see her in a dress or a skirt. Sofi was in a three-sister African print patchwork dress with blue platform shoes. She also had on a long, multi-coloured bead necklace, about six bracelets on one wrist, a charm watch-bracelet on the other and long, pink, spiral earrings. She was wearing purple lip gloss and metallic-silver eye shadow. Sofi is attracted to colour the way nails are attracted to a magnet.

All three of us have been best friends ever since kindergarten. I felt a lump build in my throat.

"So you're really going," Dede said, pulling up a chair and sitting down.

"Mmm hmm," I said, not trusting myself to speak.

"I wish you didn't have to," Sofi said. She washed her hands at the sink and started eating with me. That's how close we are. She doesn't even have to ask to be invited before she starts eating.

"I wish I didn't have to too."

"Mmm. Is this Auntie Memuna's *waakye*? Today's tastes even better than usual. Sogakofe can't be that bad, I hear they have lots of grilled tilapia there."

For Sofi, food cured every problem. She writes a fashion and food blog. It was nice to know that Sofi had heard about the local cuisine of the town. If she knew about their food, then the town couldn't be as bad as I expected it to be.

The first time I'd told my friends in school I was leaving to go to Sogakofe, Nana Ama Attakyia, a stuck-up girl in my class had asked if Sogakofe was in Togo. She and her friends had called me 'Losty' from the first day I set foot in the high school. My name, Yayra, sounds like *'ya yera'* which is Twi for 'we are lost'. Though I had explained time and time again that my name was Ewe and not Twi, Nana Ama and her friends gave me no peace.

"So who'll win the National Maths and Science Quiz for us this year?" Dede and I had both been in the maths and science club. I'm not blowing my own horn or anything but I'm really good in mathematics. I can even do some quadratic equations, differentiations and integrations in my head without working them out on paper. Last two years, though I was only in Form One; I was part of the squad my school sent for the National Maths and Science Quiz. We got all our maths answers correct. *All* of them. Daddy was so proud. He was the maths coach of the team. We've won the competition two years in a row. If we win, or rather if Higher Heights International School wins this year, they'll get to keep the trophy.

"Won't it be amazing if I get picked to join the team this year?" Dede asked.

"Amazing," Sofi said dryly and rolled her eyes. She's an

arts student. She has enough problems with core maths and can't understand how Dede and I chose additional maths over biology.

"You stand a good chance," I said ignoring Sofi.

"In my dreams," Dede said good-naturedly, "the one who stands a good chance is Bobby."

Sofi smacked her and they both turned to look at me.

It's amazing how just hearing his name caused my heart to beat faster. Bobby Laryea my boyfriend. I had had a crush on him from the first day I stepped in Higher Heights. I'd seen him only three times since the accident.

"Has he been here?" Dede asked ignoring a glare from Sofi.

I shook my head. "Maybe he's busy," I mumbled. I got up to wash my hands and dried them on my jeans. Mama had packed the napkins.

Sofi snorted.

"Busy being an idiot," Dede said under her breath, but I pretended not to hear her.

"Does he know you're leaving today?" This time it was Sofi who asked the question. She took the empty plate and rinsed it out at the sink. Mama had also packed the sponge and Sunlight liquid soap.

"He sent a WhatsApp message," I said.

Dede rolled her eyes.

Sofi asked, "Are you defending him?"

"No, he just . . . maybe it's a little too much for him. He really liked Dad and . . . maybe my face . . . maybe the way

I look . . ."

"What's *wrong* with you? *You* lost your Dad. *You* were in that accident. *You* almost died and it's a *little too much* for *him*?" Dede said.

"Can we not talk about this please?"

Dede rolled her eyes again. Sofi studied her nails. Each fingernail was painted a different colour. She hoped to be a fashion designer someday, so naturally, it was she who asked, "Have you seen your new school uniform? I hope it's cool."

"It's okay," I said, glad that she'd changed the subject. "A green pinafore with a white shirt." At Higher Heights, girls had worn navy blue skirts and light blue sleeveless shirts.

"I hope you've had it altered. You don't want to show up on your first day looking like a tree.

"Yeah, Mama had her seamstress alter it. I'm glad the shirt has sleeves."

They both nodded and I knew they understood. I hadn't worn a sleeveless dress, shirt or tank top since the accident. The looks on their faces weren't looks of pity. I had had enough of those looks from people when I got discharged from the hospital. People had looked at me with a mix of pity and sorrow. Like they hadn't known what was worse—that I had lost my Dad or that I had survived the accident looking the way I did.

"You've got to send us pictures of the school and your classroom, your new house, everything . . ." Dede said.

"I will, but only of the house and of me in the uniform. We're not allowed to have phones on the campus. It's an instant two-week suspension. It was in the rulebook that came with the prospectus."

"You can't take a phone to school?"

"Nope."

"What sort of nonrational rule is that?" Sofi asked.

"Sofi, I don't think 'nonrational' is a word," Dede said.

"Duh? 'Non' is a word. 'Rational' is a word. Nonrational *is* a word. But that's not the point. That rule is stupid."

"Well, it's their school and it's their rules and I guess you just have to abide by them. You can't wear jewellery apart from watches and stud-earrings and you can't wear nail polish or lip gloss."

"Those rules are all non—"Sofi began.

"Rational," the three of us said together and started laughing.

"I guess it's a good thing we got you this then," Dede said.

Sofi reached into her bag and brought out a blue case with a pink bow. I knew what it was before I even opened it. I removed the bow and opened the case. Nestling on a pillow inside it was a watch. It was not just any ordinary watch but a type where I could change the straps and the faces depending on the colour I wanted. There were six different coloured leather straps, six plain coloured rims and six rims inlaid with different coloured stones. I had lusted after this watch for months.

"Thank you, thank you, thank you!" I cried and hugged them both knowing they must have had to use almost all their savings to get it for me. "I've wanted this since . . . since . .

. forever!"

"We're really going to miss you," Dede whispered hugging me again. Then Sofi who was fighting hard to keep back her tears joined in and we had a three-way hug.

"Me too," I said knowing I was going to miss them more. At least they had each other. I had no one.

C h a p t e r

2

"Ready?" Mama asked.

Sofi and Dede had left. The movers had almost finished loading their truck. The house was empty. I was standing in the kitchen looking at the mango and pawpaw trees Daddy had planted in the backyard and wondering if the new family that was going to move in would keep them or cut them down.

I wondered if the kids in the family would know they could use the seeds of the flamboyant tree for a bean bag. I wondered if they'd see the broken lower branch of the mango tree and wonder what had happened to it. They wouldn't know I'd nagged Daddy for a swing when I was six. Daddy had got tired of my nagging and rigged an old tyre onto the lowest branch for me. I came home the next day with almost half my class after boasting in school about my new swing. Instead of sitting on the swing like we were supposed to, five of us had stood on it. Sofi and Dede were right there in the thick of things with me. We kept shouting for those on the ground to 'push, push' and they did. After one of their pushes, we came tumbling down like Humpty Dumpty with the broken branch falling on top of us. Luckily, we escaped with minor scrapes and bruises, but Daddy had said no more swings for me.

I wondered if they would fix the broken eaves over the back porch. If they left it the way it was, they would find out that a dove couple came to nest and lay eggs five times each year.

Mama came to stand by me. She put her hand on my shoulder. I stiffened. She took it off without saying a word and walked away. It was not that I intended hurting her, it was just that . . . that . . . I resented her for making us leave. I had grown up in this house; thrown my baby teeth onto the roof of this house; had my first pet rabbit in this house but I had forgotten to lock its cage one day. The next morning it had burrowed its way out of our compound. I had even cooked my first meal in this house and had had my first somewhat awkward kiss by the garage in this same house. But what hurt most was that leaving felt like we were leaving Daddy behind; like he didn't matter anymore; like the part of our life that had had him in it was over.

I sighed and walked through the house one last time. In each room, there was a memory that came back to me. In the living room I could picture Daddy sprawled on the sofa with his long legs hanging over the ends, remote control in his hand, engrossed in a football game. At the dining hall, he was sitting at the head of the table forcing himself to chew burnt fried plantain that I had left unattended while it was on the fire. After swallowing he had said, "This is superb; this is fantastic!"

I remembered the time I caught him eating a bar of Golden Tree chocolate in the kitchen. Mama doesn't allow us to eat sweets or unhealthy food. She would have been furious to find Daddy eating chocolate. He had hidden the bar behind him and stopped chewing when I entered.

"What are you eating?" I had asked.

"Me? Nothing?" he had mumbled with his mouth full.

"Daddy, you're lying. Open your mouth."

He had swallowed and used his tongue to run over the front of his teeth before opening it.

"What do you have in your hands?"

Daddy had brought out his right hand and showed me his empty palm. His other hand was still behind him. I had rolled my eyes. "Your other hand."

He had begun sending the right hand behind him when I said, "Keep that where I can see it." He had brought out the second hand with the barely eaten bar of chocolate.

"Larger half," I had said.

He had laughed and divided the chocolate. "That's very good." Daddy and I had this game we played where we tried to outdo each other by saying oxymora.

"I'm not just saying it for the game. I really want the larger half."

"In order to avoid a minor crisis with your Mom, I'll give

in this time," Daddy had said handing over the larger half of the chocolate.

"That's your only choice," I had said warming up to the game.

"In my unbiased opinion, you're really getting good at this game."

"You're clearly confused and I consider that seriously funny," I had said triumphantly.

The person who could use two or more oxymora in a sentence was the automatic winner. We had just finished our illicit snack when we heard Mama's car at the gate. Daddy had quickly placed the chocolate wrapper in a black polythene bag, tied the bag tight and dropped it into the dustbin. Then we had both rushed upstairs to brush our teeth. If Mama had wondered why our breaths were fresh and minty in the middle of the day, she hadn't asked. She hadn't suspected a thing.

I swallowed the lump that was forming in my throat but couldn't keep the tears from flowing down. He was gone and was never coming back and it was all my fault. I went to the bathroom and splashed water on my face. My left hand began to ache. I took two ibuprofen tablets, picked up my overnight bag and began pumping the rubber ball that the physiotherapist said was to help my fingers regain function. I walked out of the only home I'd ever known.

There was no space in the back seat of Mama's car. It was loaded with the TV set, the microwave and some other things we had used that morning. I would have no choice but to sit in the passenger seat of the car. Since the accident, I had avoided sitting in the passenger seat.

The movers were securing a tarpaulin over the back of their truck. Mama was in the garage where she had stored some boxes that had things she was giving away to a children's home. Our neighbour had promised to do that for her.

"I'm ready," I said.

"Okay. I'll go and lock up," she said, walking out of the garage. She stopped at the door and turned to look at me. "I know this is hard for you but it'll get better. I promise it will."

I shrugged. She walked away. I was about to walk away too when I noticed a jumper sticking out of one of the boxes. It was Daddy's. Mama had cleared all his things from the house before I got discharged from the hospital. She had kept some of his mathematics textbooks for me but nothing else remained of him. Not a single thing. And now here was his jumper. I went to the box and pulled it out and buried my head in it. It still carried his scent. I looked through the box and found more of his stuff, an old wallet, a sweater and some papers he had worked maths on. I picked up the box and was putting it into the car when Mama came out.

"Yayra, that's just junk," Mama said.

"I want it."

The movers had got into their truck and were driving out of the compound.

"Put it back. It's not going to bring him back."

"It's all I have left of him," I said. I was on the verge of tears. Maybe Mama saw the tears shining through my eyes so instead of insisting she just asked me to enter the car and went to shut the garage door and that's when she saw him.

"Hi Bobby, so nice of you to come say goodbye. How are your parents?"

"They're fine."

I got out of the car slowly. I didn't want him to know how really glad I was that he had come. We had been dating for over a year but I still had butterflies in my stomach anytime I saw Bobby Laryea.

"I'm taking the keys to Adjoa Maame," Mama said.

"Bobby!" I said and hugged him as soon as Mama was out of sight. I couldn't help myself. I was so happy to see him and he looked extra handsome in his jeans and Lacoste polo shirt.

"I thought you wouldn't come. I'm not even gone and I miss you so much already."

Bobby hugged me back somewhat less enthusiastically but I was too happy to notice. He let go of me and stepped back.

"This is my final year," he said.

"I know. It's come quickly hasn't it?" If the accident hadn't happened it would have been my final year too. Next year we'd have been going to University.

"I really have to study hard to get good grades."

I took his hand and squeezed it. "You'll be fine. I know you'll blow the WASSCE."

He let go of my hand and took another step back.

"I don't want any distractions—I mean I don't want to write

remedial exams or anything of that sort. I want to pass the exams one-touch."

I was on the verge of saying, "But you will, I know you will," but I didn't, not because I didn't think he would pass but because I suddenly felt uneasy.

Bobby put his hands into his pockets and looked at the ground.

O my goodness, he's breaking up with me. I stood there watching him gather courage to say the words but I still couldn't believe it was happening.

"I feel we both need a little space."

A little space for what?

"I mean, obviously, we have different priorities now. You're moving to a new place, new school, you have a lot of catching up to do with your academic work and I *need* to make sure I get all A's in the WASSCE. I *can't* afford to be distracted in any way."

A distraction? Was that what I had become? "Are you . . . are we . . . are you breaking up with me?"

"No, of course not. I'm just saying we should go on a break for some time."

"What does that mean exactly?"

"No phone calls, no e-mails, no WhatsApp messages."

I nodded like I understood. Like I'd been 'going on breaks' with boys all my life. "So how long . . . ? I mean when . . . ?"

"Let's try it till the end of first term then we will have a re-evaluation and decide if we're both headed in the same direction or if it's best to separate."

A lump formed in my throat and I suddenly found it difficult to breathe.

"You do understand, don't you?"

I didn't trust myself to speak. I nodded instead.

"Good. I knew you would." He looked relieved that I understood.

"Bobby?"

"Yeah?"

"Is this . . . are you . . . are we separating because of how I look?"

He looked away from me, scuffed the toe of his sneakers on the ground. "No, of course not."

I knew he was lying. What was more he knew I knew he was lying.

"Sofi said you had one more surgery left, right? I'm sure they'll fix you up and make you look better."

Fix me? I did have one more surgery left. But it wasn't for my face. The plastic surgeons had done all they could for me. They had even taken skin from my butt and patched it on my face. Butt-face. The surgery was to reverse my colostomy.

"Okay, take care then," he said and walked away.

I stood there not quite believing what had happened. All I could think was *no phone calls, no e-mails, no Whatsapp messages.* How was I going to survive? He met Mama at the gate and they chatted a bit. Mama was all smiles, the way she gets when everything is going according to her plan.

"Sweet of him to come by, wasn't it?" she asked as she got into the car. If she noticed the tears in my eyes, she didn't say anything. She probably thought I was on the verge of tears because I wouldn't be seeing Bobby anymore.

I slid into the passenger seat beside her. I didn't need her to tell me to buckle up. I could see her checking out of the corner of her eye to make sure I was strapped in. It wouldn't have been more obvious if she had turned around and just checked. She took a final look at the house that she had called home for twenty years and we drove off.

*

I put on my sunglaszses and stared out the window as Mama drove. It took fifteen minutes for us to move from McCarthy Hill to Tetteh Quarshie Circle. We spent another forty minutes getting to the motorway from the Tetteh Quarshie Circle. I bought a jumbo-sized bag of plantain chips from a hawker on the street, silently daring Mama to comment. She looked straight ahead as if she hadn't seen me, but to show her disapproval her lips remained in a straight line. I ripped the bag open and began munching.

Three months was not so long. By the time the first term was over, Bobby would realize just how much he had missed me and everything would be back to normal. Don't people say absence makes the heart grow fonder? Besides my birthday was in six weeks, I was sure he'd call me then. Maybe he'd even make us get together as my birthday present. On the other hand if he was freaking out because of my face, who knew what he would do if he found out about the colostomy. I sighed in despair. Mama mistook it for impatience. We'd got stuck in traffic again at the Tema motorway roundabout.

"We're making haste slowly," she said as the traffic began moving.

I pretended I had not heard her. I wasn't ready to play the oxymoron game with her. It was something special between Daddy and me. Her attempt at playing it with me felt like a violation of some sort.

Mama wouldn't give up though. "Can you give me an exact estimate of how long we've been stuck here?"

"I don't feel like playing okay?"

She nodded but I could tell she was disappointed. She switched on the radio and didn't make any more attempts at talking to me until we got to the police barrier at Tsopoli.

"Do you want to pee?"

"No."

The police stopped us at the barrier. One officer came up to us.

"Madam Doctor, are you moving?" he asked, as he glanced at her windscreen and checked her vehicle insurance and road worthiness stickers. Her medical association sticker was right beneath the other two.

"Yes, to Sogakofe."

"District hospital or Comboni?"

"The district hospital," Mama said.

"My wife comes from there. It's a nice town," he said waving for her to proceed. "Safe journey."

"Thank you," she said and continued driving. The movers were long gone. I couldn't see their truck. Most of the drivers who were behind us over took her. She slowed even more when cars approached from the opposite lane. I knew she was doing this for me. I'd been terrified of sitting in a moving car the first month after I'd been discharged from the hospital. A part of me wanted to thank her; a second part just pushed it aside. She was my mother; it was her job to take care of me.

I spent most of the journey looking out the window. Not that there was much to see—it was just grass, grass and more grass with a tree or two in between. We hardly saw people until we got to the small towns, Dawa, Sege, Koluedor, but even then there still wasn't much to see—just *trotro* stations and container-stores, a school, a church or two, sometimes a mosque and many small *atakpame* huts and a few cement block buildings.

We had been on the road for about an hour when a boy aged no more than seven or eight walked right into the middle of the road and held up his hand for us to stop. Mama slowed down reluctantly and kept peering into the bushes. I think she was afraid we were going to be robbed or something. There had been news reports of groups of armed men who pounced on travellers when they stopped on the roads.

The boy disappeared into the bushes and reappeared seconds later leading a herd of cattle. Mama visibly relaxed. The boy and two dogs guided the cows across the road. The dogs nipped at the heels of any of the cows who appeared to be straying. When the boy whistled a command to them, they either disappeared into the bush to guide more cows out or went ahead of the herd to the bushes on the other side of the road. After about five minutes when all the cows had crossed over, the young boy waved his thanks. Mama continued driving.

I dozed off. When I woke up, we were parked by the side of the road. Mama was by the roadside examining a pile of watermelons for sale. The woman selling them cut one open and offered Mama a slice. Mama was nodding at something the woman was saying as she bit into the fruit. Her eyes opened wide in surprise and she took another bite. I could tell the watermelon tasted good. Mama must have commended the woman because she beamed with pride. Mama pointed at three big ones. The woman picked them up and followed her to the car.

"Do you want a slice?" Mama asked when she noticed I was awake.

"No."

"It has lots of fibre."

I rolled my eyes. She took that as a no. She found space for them at the back and reached into her bag for her purse. The woman ran back to the heap and returned with a smaller watermelon.

"Madam, your *ntosuoɔ*," she said.

Mama thanked her and we left. For the next stretch of the

journey instead of abandoned grassland there were fields of watermelon on both sides of the road. They were different sizes, most oval or round, some were deep green others were a lighter green with white stripes. They just lay there, with no fence or guard or anything just a bunch of scarecrows, some of which looked almost human with their billowing trousers, flapping shirts and floppy hats.

Other fields had pepper plants with long, red peppers hanging from them. They looked beautiful and added more colour to the green landscape. Some of the peppers had already been harvested and had been spread to dry on black plastic sheets by the roadside.

There were more piles of watermelon and more sellers by the roadside the further we moved from Accra. They flagged us each time we passed by. Other sellers had tables that had baskets of juicy yellow mangoes, red and purple *saloon* mangoes, bundles of shallots, crates of red, ripe tomatoes and sacks of rock salt.

We drove past two boys who were unloading a wagon of watermelons by the road.

"Remember how Da—"

"Yes," I snapped before Mama could finish her sentence. She looked at me and sighed. I continued looking out the window. I couldn't believe that Mama didn't know that it was because I remembered everything about Daddy that letting go of him was so difficult. She had been about to ask if I remembered how Daddy used to chew the watermelon seeds. He never spat them out. He said they were the best part of the fruit. He said it tasted like eating watermelon with roast groundnuts. I tried it once. The seeds were crunchy I admit but to me they had no taste.

"I'm trying my best. I really am," Mama said quietly.

She didn't speak to me after that. Not even when we got to Ada. I saw her glance at the turn-off that led to the beach. She gripped the wheel tightly and bit her lip. I knew she remembered the last time we had gone there. It had been right after we won the National Maths and Science Quiz.

We had spent the weekend at a resort by the Ada beach. We had had a lovely time. The beach was clean; cleaner than any beach in Accra that I'd been to. We'd hired a boat that had taken us on a tour of the river. We had gone as far as the Sogakofe Bridge, but at that time none of us had known Sogakofe would come to play a major part in our lives. From the bridge we had gone to the estuary. Being at the estuary had been scary. It was almost as if the river and sea were fighting. The waves were turbulent and loud. The tour guide said the river and the sea both had spirits and that the sea spirit didn't like the river spirit entering it. He told us fisher folk had to offer regular sacrifices to the sea spirit to appease it. He told us stories of fishermen who had seen *Mami wata* and *Papa wata* relaxing on the beach while they took their canoes to sea.

We had gone back to Accra on a Sunday. Bobby had been on his way out of our yard when we arrived. Bobby. I tried to keep the tears away when I remembered we were 'on a break'. He had come to congratulate me. As the only junior who had joined the senior team I had suddenly become famous in school. People who had never said one word to me had all started acting like we had been best friends for ages. Even people who had teased me about my name, asking "You and who are lost?" anytime I said my name, were civil to me; even Nana Ama Attakyia who had called me 'Losty' since my first day in senior high.

Bobby had invited me to watch a movie with him at the mall. I had rushed inside to ask Daddy and Mama if I could go. They had both agreed. One outing had led to another and then to another and by the time school had reopened for our second year, Bobby and I were officially a couple and I had had my first and only kiss with him by our garage door. Two months after school reopened Daddy and I had had the accident. I had been out of school for the rest of the school year. Now, Bobby, Dede and Sofi were all my seniors and I was about to begin my second year with a group of juniors in a place I didn't know.

Mama didn't make any more stops and she didn't ask me any more questions either. The stretches of grassland between the towns were not as long as before and there were more vehicles and people on the road. I tried to go back to sleep but I couldn't. I put my earphones in my ears and switched on my iPod.

One town we entered had pots for sale everywhere—different colours, different shapes, different sizes. I loved their colours and sizes. They were beautiful; things you'd see on display in offices and fancy restaurants. I gasped and Mama turned to look at me. She had driven to Sogakofe several times to make arrangements for her job and my new school and I think she had become used to the sight.

She pulled out the earpiece in my left ear. "Do you want us to stop? We could buy a couple."

I shrugged as if I didn't care if she continued driving or stopped but I did want her to stop. I looked in the side mirror as we drove past the last stall. She caught me looking and stopped on the shoulder of the road. She waited for a tractor to drive past us and did a U-turn.

"I could use a break. Let's stretch our legs a bit, shall we?" Without waiting for me to reply, she picked her handbag and got out of the car. I followed her out, trying to pretend I didn't care that she had stopped but I couldn't resist walking up to a stand and just staring at the pots and vases. It was almost like they had some power over me. I passed my hand over one of the vases. It was as smooth as glass.

The young man whose stand it was came to stand by me. "You have good eyes. That one is fine *paa*. Only that one remain. The clay they use make am no be common. You have to go far far away to get am. That one be the last one."

"It's beautiful," Mama said.

"Mmm hmm. It looks like glass, doesn't it?" I said and rubbed my hand over the red vase.

"It does," Mama said, looking at me and probably realizing that this was the first time I had agreed with her on anything since Daddy died.

"How much?" she asked the young man eager to make our 'moment' last.

I left her haggling over the price with the young man and walked to the next stall hoping to find more of the beautiful vases. There weren't any others like it, but there were several more pots. Some almost came up to my waist. Others were so small they fitted into the palm of my hand. I was still browsing through the stalls when I heard Mama honk. I left the pots reluctantly and walked back to the car.

"I'm paying the movers by the hour. We'll come back another time, okay?"

"Okay. Thanks for the vase."

"You're welcome," she said. I could see she wanted to say more. A whole lot more but she kept quiet. I put my earpieces back in.

In no time at all we were at the Sogakofe Bridge. The River Volta flowed calmly beneath it. 'Lower Volta Bridge,' the sign before the bridge said. Next to it were about ten empty yellow sheds and a sign that said 'fish market'. There was no going back now. We had arrived.

*

Once we got across the bridge, bread, biscuit, *aboloo*, fried yam, fried oyster and *chofi* sellers all stuck their wares through the open car windows hoping to tempt us to buy some. Mama drove right through them.

People on motorbikes zoomed past us. Sometimes there were as many as four people on a bike, none of whom wore helmets. What surprised me was that the passengers were women with babies strapped to their backs or toddlers whom they placed between themselves and the drivers. It looked like the *okada* business was really booming.

At the roundabout I saw a signboard for my new school. Mama kept driving until I saw another one for the hospital. Not long after that we drove into the hospital compound. The security man, who had obviously met Mama before, greeted her profusely. He practically stuck his neck into the car so he could see me too.

Mama introduced me. "This is my daughter, Yayra Amenyo."

"Yayra. *O* nice, nice. I am Mr Lucky Agbesi. You're very welcome."

"Thank you," I said.

There was a row of cream and green coloured bungalows a little distance away from the main hospital building. The movers were already unpacking when we got there. Our belongings lay scattered on the front lawn.

"Isn't the door open?" Mama asked getting out of the car.

"No, madam."

"Are you sure?" she got down and checked. She turned the knob this way and that but the door wouldn't budge. She went to the back of the house. I looked around and noticed two boys weeding in the yard next to ours. The older, taller one was faster. His plot looked leveller and neater. The younger one had stopped to stare at us. At a word from the older boy he continued weeding. Mama came back, took her phone from her bag and dialled a number. I could see the call was not going through.

"Madam, we finish *o*," one of the movers called out.

Mama was in near panic mode; things were not going according to her plan. "But you just can't leave. You have to send the things inside."

"Madam, we get another job we for do today."

"Please . . .," Mama said.

"Okay, we go wait ten minutes."

"Thank you," Mama said. She tried calling one more time but still couldn't get through. She turned and noticed the boys.

"Hey! Hey!" she called.

Both boys stood up and looked at her. Come, she motioned with her hand.

I think the taller boy told the younger to continue weeding. He dropped his cutlass and pulled out a handkerchief. Instead of going back to work, the younger just stood watching. He used it to wipe his face and sauntered over to Mama. He didn't even glance my way. His eyes were on the vase, which I had placed by one of the walls.

"Umm, *medekuku*, administrator . . .," Mama began then she turned to me. "How do you say 'house' in Ewe?"

I shrugged. Mama was Akan, Daddy was Ewe. I'd grown up speaking Twi.

She turned back to the boy, "Administrator *hɔmɛ*?"

A wary look passed over his face. I thought people in small towns and villages were always falling over themselves to make others feel welcome. "I speak English and Twi," the boy said.

"Oh, thank God. Do you know which one is the administrator's house?"

The boy pointed to one of the bungalows.

"Thank you. Thank you." She turned and started walking in that direction.

"He's not home," the boy called after her.

"Where's he gone?" Mama asked.

The boy shrugged.

"When's he coming back?"

Another shrug. He turned and ambled back to the plot he had been weeding.

Mama was near boiling point now. Things were so not going according to plan. She whipped the phone out of her bag once more and tried the administrator's number. This time she managed to get through. She walked away from us. You didn't need to be psychic to see she was very pissed off.

"You're where?"

The person on the line said something.

"Where's that?" she asked.

"How long will it take you to get here?"

"What? Forty-five minutes to an hour? Isn't there a spare key?"

An hour. That would be like two or three hours Ghana time. Apparently the movers thought the same thing. When Mama ended her call they told her they couldn't wait that long. Mama paid them and they left.

"He said he forgot! Can you believe that? And yet I called him this morning!" she said coming to sit by me on the veranda. I was eating the rest of the plantain chips.

"Are you hungry? We might as well go and get something to eat," she said looking at her watch.

"I'm okay," I said.

"I'm starving. I'll get us some food. Look after the things will you?" An order. Not a question or a request. She got into the car and drove away.

*

I walked around my new home. It seemed strange to be calling it a home without Daddy. The two boys continued weeding. They ignored me totally, which was just fine by me. I wondered if they were our neighbours.

Our lawn had been weeded. There was a patch of burnt grass at the back where I assumed the cut grass had been burned. There were two mango trees behind the building. Both of them were in bloom and bore inflorescences of little greenish pink and yellow flowers and very tiny green mango fruits. The air smelled heavenly. I wondered if they'd be *saloon* mangoes or regular mangoes. I hoped they would be the *saloon* type but I wasn't holding my breath.

Drying lines had been strung between the two trees. An army of red ants marched up and down the rough bark. I went closer to the trees hoping to catch a better whiff. There was an angry cackle and a flock of guinea fowls came flying down the tree and began running helter skelter. I was so scared I screamed then immediately regretted it. The two boys in the adjacent yard looked at me. The older boy said something to the younger one and they both laughed. I felt so stupid. He had probably said something like "Silly city girl afraid of guinea fowls".

I went back to the front and sat down in a corner of the veranda wondering what was taking Mama so long. Had she got lost? As if she could read my thoughts she called.

"They're making everything from scratch. Can you believe that? I asked how long it would take before I placed my order, and the waiter said '*O*, not long, like ten minutes' and I believed him. Turns out they are now grilling the fish and boiling the rice!"

I could imagine her at the eatery. Probably drumming her fingers impatiently on the table top. My mother hated to be kept waiting. It drove her almost insane.

"Do you want me to come get you?"

"No, I'm fine."

"Okay, see you soon."

I was still waiting when a blue Nissan Sunny drove up to our yard. The car had barely come to a stop before the driver got out and came running to the veranda.

"I am so so sorry. You must be Yayra, I am Wonder Dugbenu, the administrator. I hope I haven't kept you waiting long. Where is Dr Sarpong?" To his credit he didn't stare at me longer than was necessary.

"She went to get us lunch . . . or supper," I said looking up. The sun had begun setting.

"*O*, this is not good. Not good at all. First impressions and I forget the key! I am so sorry," he said, moving towards the door with the key. He opened it and I followed him in.

"This is the hall, over there is the kitchen. Store room there, master bedroom and two bedrooms down the corridor. There's only one bathroom and toilet, though, and no dining area, I'm afraid," he said looking at me. Like it mattered to me whether or not there was a dining room.

"It's okay. I usually eat in my bedroom."

"Good, good. Now let's get these things inside before Dr Sarpong gets back. Just tell me where you want them to go."

We moved the living room furniture in first. Then he went outside and grabbed a box. Mama being Mama she had labelled all the boxes. The label on it said 'kitchen'. I followed him in with my overnight bag and my vase which I placed on the centre table. I went to check out the two bedrooms. They were both the same size, both had a double wardrobe and a full length mirror. I chose the one farther away from the master bedroom so that I could truthfully say I didn't hear Mama when she called.

I was going back outside when I met the younger boy in the hall. He didn't see me at first so he lost his balance and let out a scream when he did see me. He bumped into the centre table and my vase crashed to the ground.

"What happened? What broke?" I heard Mama call. She stood in the doorway with two white polythene bags in her hand. I could see the outline of the takeout packs in the bags. She placed the bags on one of the sofas.

The boy looked from her to me. He was scared. "I'm sorry. It was an accident."

Mr Dugbenu and the older boy appeared behind Mama. They were carrying the fridge.

"We just got that!" Mama screamed. "Yayra just picked that

on our way here and you broke it!"

The younger boy cowered in fear. The older one scowled. Mr Dugbenu looked like he'd rather be anywhere than where he was right then.

"I'll replace it," the older boy said looking from Mama to me. I felt his gaze travel over my face and settle on the left half. I looked away.

"How?" Mama asked. "They said that was the last one left; that they get the clay from some faraway place."

"Mama, it's okay. It's just a vase," I said.

"No, it's not okay," she screamed.

She looked at the broken pieces on the floor and said softly, "What are we doing here? Why did I bring you here? What was I thinking?"

I almost felt sorry for her. Almost. She exhaled and covered her face with her hands. Then she walked past me and went out through the back door.

The room went quiet. Mr Dugbenu and the tall boy put the fridge down. All three of them looked at me. I know they expected me to go after her but I did not. I went to my room and shut the door hard letting her know that the fact that she was having second thoughts about bringing us here did not absolve her of anything.

Chapter

4

I heard Mama go back into the living room. I don't know what she told the administrator or the boys and I didn't much care. I heard them bring in more stuff with Mama giving instructions, "Just leave that there for now", "I'll look through later", "That should go to the storeroom". They left my things in front of my door. I heard them coming and going, moving through the house. I heard them hammering and knocking things into place. They assembled my bed but left it outside the door. They assembled Mama's bed too.

They finished bringing in everything at 9 p.m. I heard Mama thank the boys and the administrator profusely for their help. She told them to forget about replacing the vase. Any other person I know would have called it a night. Anyone else would have been exhausted from the move, the drive and the packing, anyone else but not Mama. Mama isn't anyone. The plan had been to put everything away today and she would make sure it was all done so she could tick it off her list before she went to bed. She started unpacking right away. I knew it was too much work for one person but I also knew Mama would be able to do it all without asking me for help.

The only reason I left my room later that night was because I was hungry and thirsty. I found her in the kitchen, putting the plates and pans away. She barely looked up when I entered. She pointed at the microwave, which she had found a space for on top of one of the counters. It was already plugged into a socket. In the microwave was one of the takeout packs she had brought in earlier. I transferred the food onto a plate and heated it.

"There's juice in the fridge," she said when the microwave beeped.

I carried my plate of vegetable rice, grilled tilapia and glass of pineapple juice to my room. After eating, I dragged my mattress in and placed it on the floor. I changed my colostomy bag, brushed my teeth and washed my face. I was so tired I didn't even do that properly. I only managed to remove my jeans before I collapsed onto the mattress. In minutes I was dead to the world. I vaguely remember Mama coming in and covering me with a cloth but at the time I thought I was dreaming.

*

"Kicks coming up in three . . . two . . . one . . . and kick . . . kick . . . kick. There you go! Remember to suck in your belly to your spine. Make sure your hips and shoulders are aligned. That's the perfect spinal alignment. I want you to stand tall and walk tall. Great posture is so important! Kick . . . kick . . . kick."

I woke up to the sound of Mama's aerobics instructor. It was past noon. I knew exactly where I was and the sinking feeling I had had the previous day returned. My phone beeped. A WhatsApp message.

Hey girl ☺ watz up? How's Soga? Y r u nt replyng?

It was a new message from Sofi. She and Dede had already sent seven messages.

Just woke up. Will call l8r.

I got out of bed and went to pee. The door to Mama's room was open. She waved when she saw me.

"Sleep well?"

"Okay."

"We'll pass by your uncle's house later, okay?" she panted. Sweat dripped down her face.

I shrugged and went back to my room. She wasn't expecting an answer from me because she hadn't asked a question. She had simply informed me of where I would be and what we would be doing later that day. That was the plan for the day.

I dragged in my suitcase and started unpacking my clothes. When Mama finished her work-out she helped me drag in my bed. She went to take a shower while I finished unpacking my clothes, shoes and books.

Three hours later we were on the road to my uncle's house. I could count the number of times I had met this uncle on one hand. One of my father's traditions had been to travel to his hometown every Easter holiday and occasionally for weekends or entire weeks when there was a funeral or some other family gathering. Mama and I never went with him. He had said we would feel left out because we didn't speak Ewe.

Mama pulled up in front of a house that was by the banks of the river. A man and woman came out of the house before we got out of the car. I had seen my uncle briefly during Daddy's funeral. He looked like a fatter version of Daddy. He was completely bald. He approached us with outstretched arms and a huge smile on his face.

"*Mia woezor loo*!" he called out.

"*Yoo*," Mama said laughing and I could see her relax.

My uncle enfolded her in a hug. Then it was the turn of the woman who was by his side. I assumed she was his wife.

"Yayra *efɔ*?" he asked and hugged me too.

I looked to Mama who translated, "How are you?"

"I'm fine," I said to my uncle.

"You say '*Ee*'," my aunt said.

"Now that you are here you have to learn the language *o*. Your father did not try *koraa*. But we will teach you. In one year you will be rattling Ewe like water, okay?"

I nodded.

"Good, good. Let's go inside," he said, leading the way into their house.

Once we were seated indoors, my aunt got us water to drink. I might not have known how to speak Ewe but I knew it would be rude to refuse to drink. That was a universal Ghanaian tradition.

I took a sip from my glass. Mama emptied her glass. She was a firm advocate of regenerative health—food is medicine; water is medicine; sleep is medicine; rest is medicine and even exercise is medicine. I could hear Edem's 'Over again', playing from somewhere farther in the house.

"*Yoo*, you are welcome. Our home is peaceful," my uncle said when my aunt came back after taking the glasses away.

"We just wanted you to know we have arrived. We came yesterday," Mama said.

"We thank God," uncle said. Then he turned to me, "Do you know me?" He didn't even wait for an answer before going on.

"I'm your uncle, Larweh, your father's older brother. This is my wife, Daavi Charity. Everyone calls her Auntie Cee. We couldn't get to talk to you much after the funeral. You are very welcome here. If you need anything, anything at all, let us know. You are our daughter."

Auntie Cee who all this while had been beaming at me said "Your cousin, Sam, is in his room studying. He's not very good at maths so Efo said he better start revising before school starts tomorrow. He's also at Sogasco. You can go and say hello."

I got up and went in the direction of the music. I heard Uncle Larweh telling Mama about his fish farm.

The music led to a room with a poster of a skull with headphones on the door. A notice in a scrawny scrawl said 'BOYS ZONE. NO GIRLS ALLOWED. NO TRESPASSING'. Another notice, this one done with a black marker proclaimed 'DJ SAMSIZZLE'. I knocked twice on the door. I didn't hear a response. I knocked a third time but even if there had been a response, I wouldn't have heard it above Edem's rapping.

I turned the handle and pushed open the door. The sound almost blew me away. There were two mega sound speakers stacked one on top of the other in a corner of the room. Clothes spilled out of a wardrobe in another corner. There were clothes everywhere—on the floor, over the doors of the wardrobes, draped over the chair by the desk and on the bed—or rather under the prone figure of DJ Samsizzle, who was fast asleep. An Aki-Ola core mathematics textbook covered his face. No wonder he was asleep. How do you read mathematics? If his strategy for learning maths was to 'chew and pour' the examples in the textbook, it was no wonder he was failing. Maths was logical, step A followed by step B. You just had to understand the steps.

Emanating from underneath the textbook were gigantic snores. I took the chance to look around DJ Samsizzle's room some more. Amidst the clothes were a couple of textbooks that looked like they hadn't been touched throughout the holidays. They were covered in a film of dust. A stack of dirty plates lay beside the bed. There were two things that were perfectly arranged. One was a shoe rack. On the top rack were four pairs of sneakers that had been placed in transparent polythene bags. The second rack had three pairs of scuffed sneakers. On the third rack were one pair of black and one pair of brown dress shoes. Not a speck of dust was to be seen on either. There were four pairs of sandals on the last rack. Two black, two brown.

The second thing that was well arranged was a CD rack that occupied one wall of the room. I went closer to read the labels. DJ Samsizzle had more CDs than I had seen in any music shop. On the desk was a desk top computer and beside it sat—I couldn't believe it, a device like Mama and Daddy's old gramophone. Seriously, who used records in this day and age? My parents had old Osibisa and Wulomei records that they used to play on a gramophone when I was younger. But the stylus had broken and they hadn't got anyone to fix it. I put my finger on the record and it stopped spinning and made a screeching sound. The snoring stopped immediately.

"Hey, don't touch that! Didn't you read the sign? No girls allowed!" Samuel said, springing up and appearing by my side.

He stopped the machine, held it up to the light and examined it. When he was satisfied that I hadn't damaged the record he put it down gently like it was an egg. Then he turned to look at me.

"How did you get in anyway?"

I pointed to the door.

He rubbed the stubble on his chin then his eyes lit up in recognition. "Hey, you're the Accra chick, my cousin, right?"

I rolled my eyes. In Accra, they called me 'Losty'. In Sogakofe were they going to call me the 'Accra chick'? "My name is Yayra and I . . .".

"I know who you are," he said leading the way out. "I'm sorry about your father."

He didn't make the pity face, so I was emboldened to ask.

"Did you know him? He was here last Easter."

"Yeah, I met him a couple of times like at funerals and things but never at Easter and not in Sogakofe."

"That can't be right. He's been coming to spend Easter in Sogakofe for as long as I can remember."

Sam shrugged, obviously not interested in the conversation. "Whatever. I'm hungry, let's go and get something to eat."

I followed him to their kitchen. He opened the fridge and brought out two bottles of coke. He stuck the mouth of the bottle into his mouth and a second later he had uncorked it with his teeth.

"Uh, Samuel, you really shouldn't use your teeth . . ."

"The name is DJ Samsizzle or just DJ. No Samuel. No Sammy. No Sam. I'm going to be a turntablist."

He handed me the bottle, repeated the process with the second bottle and took a big swig.

"What? Haven't you seen anyone do that before?" He reached back into the fridge and brought out two bowls. One had *aboloo*, the other had one-man-thousand fish.

He didn't look like he was going to offer me a glass. I wiped the mouth of my bottle with a corner of my t-shirt and took a swig. "What's a turntablist?"

He had been in the process of putting a piece of *aboloo* smothered in one-man-thousand fish in his mouth when he stopped.

"You don't know who a turntablist is? What hole did you crawl out of?"

At the confused look on my face, he shook his head and said, "The Asantes say their ancestors crawled out of a hole. You do know that, don't you?"

I shook my head.

He looked at me like I was from another planet. "Ei, Accra chick, don't you know *anything*?"

He heaped a plate with cold *aboloo*, one-man thousand fish and some *shitɔ* from a jar on the kitchen cabinet and led the way back to his room.

"This here is a turntable," he said putting the plate on the desk. "A turntablist is someone who uses turntables to make music."

"You mean like a DJ?"

He lifted his hands in frustration.

"A DJ *just* plays music. A turntablist *makes* music. There's a *huge* difference."

He wiped his hands on his shorts, put the stylus back on the record on the turntable and turned the volume up. Edem's voice filled the room once more. Just before he got to the chorus, 'I no dey fear what they say, anything I go pay . . .' DJ put two fingers on the record and started sliding them across. It was almost as if DJ had added more percussionists and drummers to the song just by sliding his fingers across. It was amazing.

"How do you do that?"

DJ looked at me and I could tell he was proud. "A turntablist uses the turntable like it's a musical instrument."

In-between mouthfuls, he spent the next ten minutes

explaining the basics of scratching, drumming and beat juggling. I just watched with my mouth wide open.

"Wow, I didn't know any of this even existed."

"I used to spin for people—you know parties, out-doorings, those kinds of things but my parents said I was not focusing on school work and made me stop."

"That's too bad, you're really good."

"Nah, you should hear some of the guys from Tema. They're wicked and they've got more sophisticated machines. They can scratch two or three records at a time. They are like absolutely wicked!"

"I'd love to see that."

He looked at me out of the corner of his eye, like he was debating whether or not to tell me something. He walked over to his bed and lifted the mattress. He dug his hand underneath it, brought out a flyer and handed it to me.

"There's a competition in two months. It's in Tema. My parents would kill me if they find out I've entered. Popee says no more spinning till my grades improve and I'm trying, I really am, but I just keep failing maths."

"I can help you."

He looked at me. "I know you're doing add maths, but Popee says you spent only two months in school last year. He says you have to repeat Form Two."

"I do have to repeat Form Two but I'm really good at maths. I'll teach you if you stop calling me 'Accra chick' and if you'll take me to this Tema competition."

He looked at me as if he was having a hard time deciding but I knew he would agree.

"Okay, deal." He offered his hand and I shook it.

Afterwards we went to join our parents by the riverbank where Uncle Larweh was showing Mama their fish farm. Auntie Cee sent us home with five fresh tilapias from their farm.

Chapter 5

"Give me two minutes of boosted walking! That's it. Remember boosted walking is jogging! Let's do this! And one . . . and two . . . and three . . ."

I rolled over and went back to sleep. I still had an hour before day broke. By the time I woke up for my first day in my new school, Mama had already finished her aerobics and was dressing up for work. She appeared in my room with two sets of outfits on hangers. One was a purple skirt suit, the other a dark blue formal peplum dress.

"Which do you think?"

I pointed to the skirt suit.

Daddy had always liked her in skirt suits. Satisfied with my choice Mama went to continue getting ready. I got ready and took pictures with my phone, which I whatsapped to Dede and Sofi.

Luking gr8! Dede sent back.

Aww, so sweet. U da bomb! Sofi replied.

"I'm ready when you are," Mama said.

I grabbed my school bag and followed her out of the door. She gave me a spare key.

"I don't want you to take me," I said.

"But why? It's your first day and you don't even know the way."

"DJ . . . Sam said it was not far from the roundabout."

"Yayra . . ."

"Mama everyone will think I'm a *dadaba* or something."

"Okay, Okay," she said but I could tell she was not pleased. "How about if you go with the hospital bus? It leaves at 7: 30 a.m. to pick up staff for the morning shift. The driver can drop you at the roundabout and pick you up in the afternoons when he goes for the afternoon staff. How about that?"

I nodded.

She drove us to the hospital car park where she introduced me to the driver, who dropped me at the roundabout. It was not difficult finding the school. I just followed the students who were dressed like I was. The road leading up to the school gates was lined with flamboyant trees. They formed a canopy over the road. It really looked pretty since the trees were in bloom. Some flowers had fallen to the ground, so the street looked like a red carpet had been laid out for us. At the school gate was an arch with the school motto: *No cross, no crown.* I knew I would fit right in. I knew all about bearing crosses.

More trees lined the road leading to the administration block. On either side of the street were arboretums. The scientific and local names of the trees had been written on boards and stuck in front of them along with the names of a group of students who had planted them and the year in which the planting was done. I thought it wasn't for nothing that their school uniform was green; they seemed to be very eco-friendly. The commonest tree was the *Gmelina arborea*. Maybe someone had made a donation to the school, or they'd got the seedlings at a cheap price or something.

There were sculptures on stumps of trees that had been felled. Each one bore the name of the student who had sculpted the work and the year in which the work had been finished. The sculptures were really good; most of them were of students doing various school activities. The one I liked most was a row of three monkey heads depicting 'See no evil, hear no evil and speak no evil'. Some other stumps were still in the process of being sculpted and I couldn't tell yet what form the finished products were going to take.

Everyone was heading to the assembly hall, so I followed them there. I kept looking around to see if I could find DJ but I couldn't. There were just too many students. The number must have been triple that of Higher Heights.

Most adults pretend that they don't know there's a social hierarchy in schools, but there is. The minute I stepped in the assembly hall I could make out the various levels. There were the athletes; you couldn't mistake their swagger for anything else. If you did indeed miss their swagger, you were sure to pick them out by their low-lying shorts belted at the mid-line of their backsides. Then there were the students who had future scholarly or judicial ambitions. They were the ones whose school bags looked like the entire A-Z of the encyclopaedia was stuffed into them. The popular girls had a distinctive look too. Their belts were not on their waists but lying around their hips. Their hair had been brushed back and scarfed so you could see the curls. Though the rule book had said no lip gloss or nail polish, I did see a few girls whose lips looked glossy and whose nails had a fine sheen to them.

All around me people exchanged hugs and high fives as they met friends they hadn't seen over the vacation. The assembly hall buzzed as people caught up on the latest news. A group of giggling girls, two rows ahead of me had their heads buried in the pages of *Ovation*. I took out my rubber ball, began pumping and settled to wait.

At exactly 8:00 a.m. a line of teachers entered the auditorium.

"Mari Jata is coming," someone whispered and the auditorium began to quieten down. Everyone got up. I got up too. After the teachers sat down, we all took our seats. A teacher walked up to the podium and welcomed everyone back to school. He had a neck as thick as a cow's. It didn't surprise me that instead of cheeks he had jowls. He looked like a cross between a horse and an ox. I felt that if he exhaled too deeply his shirt would rip open. Classes hadn't even begun and he looked like he needed another vacation. He led us in saying the Lord's Prayer and in singing both the national and the school anthems. I found out later his name was Mr Amedoda and that he was the assistant headmaster. He was also the one who caned students when corporal punishment had to be meted out.

Afterwards he introduced the headmistress. She walked up to the podium in a grey skirt suit that must have been two sizes too big. The suit seemed to hover around her body. Everyone could see it had shoulder pads. She stood on the podium in her hovering suit until there was absolute silence in the hall. I saw people sit up straighter and stop fidgeting when she looked their way. No one had to tell me she was not a woman to mess with.

"For those of you who are new here, my name is Madam Marie Yevutsey. In this school we value discipline and hard work. We do not tolerate lateness, tomfoolery or stupidity." Madam Yevutsey continued speaking for about forty-five minutes and the auditorium remained as quiet as a cemetery. She went through all the rules in the rule book from the first page to the last so that no one could claim ignorance of the rules.

The ones that applied to me as a day student were:

1. Students were not allowed to alter their uniforms in any way (I had already broken that rule and so had everyone else).

2. Students, especially female students, were not allowed to apply chemicals to their hair. Males were not supposed to cut their hair so low that the scalp showed.

3. Nails were to be cut short and were not allowed to be painted. No lip shine, gloss or make-up of any form, or jewellery apart from stud earrings and wristwatches were allowed.

4. Students were supposed to stand, smile and look at the faces of teachers before greeting them.

5. Fighting was not tolerated on or off the school campus.

6. Morning assembly was compulsory for all students.

7. Day students were not allowed on the school campus during non-teaching hours.

8. Students were to conduct themselves in an orderly manner, both within the campus and elsewhere.

9. Lateness to any school function was inexcusable.

10. Students were only allowed to call teachers by their surnames, never by nicknames or first names.

11. Speaking Ewe, pidgin English or any other vernacular was prohibited on the school compound.

12. Students were not to make unnecessary noise on the school compound.

13. Students were not to possess or use mobile phones, cameras or any music playing devices.

14. Students were to do punishments given to them by prefects and teachers before they complained.

15. Students were expected to exercise common sense at all times. A breach of common sense was a breach of school rules for which the student would be liable

to punishment. Students were to bear in mind that ignorance of the law was not an excuse.

"A word to the wise is . . ." Madam Yevutsey said.

"Enough," the student body chorused.

I could see why they called her 'Mari Jata', she was to be feared. She hadn't even smiled once since she entered the auditorium. A few teachers spoke after Mari Jata took her seat. The new students were asked to wait behind and the rest of the school was dismissed.

The boarders were sent to their respective houses to meet with their house masters and house mistresses. The day students were sent to the administration block where we presented our admission letters and receipts of fee payments to the school administrator. She produced a timetable for my class and had one of the prefects take me to the form two science block.

Class had already started when I entered. The prefect spoke to the teacher who asked me take a seat. I could feel all eyes on me. There were two vacant seats—one right in front, the other way at the back. The whispering began as I walked to the back of the class. I heard someone whisper 'Dr Blight', someone else snickered. My face grew hot as I remembered Dr Blight from the Captain Planet cartoon. She had worn her hair over one side of her face to hide a horrible scar also on the left side of her face.

The teacher whose name I didn't get said, "This is Yayra Amenyo. She'll be joining us for the rest of the year."

It was a maths class and he was teaching quadratic equations, something I could do with my eyes closed. Whenever the teacher turned his back, people turned and stared openly at me. You'd have thought I was some kind of freak on display.

"What happened to her face?" someone whispered.

"Don't know, don't care," the person he was talking to whispered back.

I pretended that I hadn't heard and kept my head up though I felt tears pricking the back of my eyes.

After the class, one boy yelled, "Hey new girl, what happened to your face?"

It wasn't as easy to pretend I hadn't heard.

"Car accident," I said.

"Shoulda worn your seatbelt," he said and turned back to his book.

The second lesson was chemistry. I tried to pay attention but soon gave up. At break time, a group of girls walked out together. One of them turned and looked at me. She said something to the other two who both turned and giggled.

"Dr Blight, no break for you?"

I ignored them. In high school hierarchy, they are the popular girls, the girls who come from rich families and look down on anyone who isn't like them. Usually that included people who didn't go to a particular group of junior high school; or who don't live in a particular area; or who don't attend a particular kind of church or mosque; or shop or hang out at all the popular places. They are the Nana Ama Attakyia's of the world. There's at least one of them in each school. Now I had three of them in my class. They were still giggling when a boy walked past them.

"Hey, Vampire! How were your holidays?" the girl in the middle called out.

A second girl asked, "Did you drink lots of human blood?"

The boy glared at them and walked out. The three girls left the classroom giggling. I remained on my seat while people left in twos and threes.

When the classroom was totally empty I took out my phone. I knew it was against the rules but I had known there would be no way I'd get through my first day without seeing my father's face. There was no way I'd survive the day without hearing his voice, without hearing him laugh.

I played one of the videos I had taken of him at home dancing and singing along to Kojo Antwi's *Tom and Jerry Awareε*. My Dad was a fantastic dancer. He could twist and turn in any which way—we used to dance together all the time. He just had to hear a tune and he'd be on his feet.

"Happily married," I had called out from behind the camera.

"What?"

"An oxymoron—happily married."

He had slowed down his steps as he continued dancing but he considered it for a minute and said, "Nah."

"Why not?"

"Well, because most people *are* happily married."

"Are you?"

"Am I what?"

"Are you happily married?"

He had stopped dancing and turned to look at me. I had zoomed in to capture his face. He had suddenly looked very serious.

"Of course I'm happily married. What makes you ask that?"

"Nothing."

"You sure?"

"Yup."

"Did your mother say anything to you?"

"About what?" I had asked beginning to feel uncomfortable. Had they been fighting?

"I love you and your mother very much, okay? Don't ever forget that."

"Are you like dying or something? Do you like have cancer or some incurable disease?"

"Hey, can't I tell my own daughter that I love her? When did that become a crime?"

"I didn't mean . . ."

"Never mind. Come and join me," he had said offering his hand to me. The video showed a portion of the ceiling as I put the phone down and danced with him. After about thirty seconds of showing the ceiling the screen went blank.

I switched off the phone when I heard students coming into the classroom. They were speaking Pidgin English. I sighed in relief as DJ Samsizzle and another boy entered. Both of them wore their shorts lying low on their buttocks. DJ was in one of the sneakers that had been in the transparent polythene bags. His companion wore a similar brand of sneakers.

"I couldn't find you at the snack square. Aren't you hungry?" DJ asked.

I shook my head.

"My cuson dat," he told the boy reverting to Pidgin English.

"Be like I know am somwhere," the boy said staring at me.

"Shun fool. If you mess with am, I go make you know," DJ said and smacked the boy's head.

"No for real. I see am before for somplace," the boy insisted.

"Padiman, you for dey g," DJ warned.

"I no dey lie. I see am before."

DJ snorted, "Apuu! The chick plus im Momee land on Saturday. Yesterdee dem come ma dere. Where you meet am for?"

I was beginning to feel uncomfortable. Was he also going to say I reminded him of Dr Blight?

"Maybe you've mistaken me for someone else."

"No, I never forget a face . . . I'm sure it will come to me. Sorry if I made you feel uncomfortable. My name is Mawuko Kosidem but everyone calls me—"

"Gbagladza," he and DJ said together and gave each other high fives.

I knew what *gbagbladza* meant. Daddy had been terrified of cockroaches. He used to shout *'gbagbladza, gbagbladza'* anytime he saw a cockroach and jumped on a chair or table until Mama and I came and killed it. I had no idea why a grown man would be afraid or cockroaches. I also had no idea why anyone would name himself after a cockroach.

"I'm Yayra Amenyo," I said and offered my hand.

"Blessing. That's a pretty name."

For the first time since I'd entered the school compound I felt better. For the first time in my life no one had made any wisecracks about my name. For the first time in my life I felt proud of my name and felt like I belonged.

"What's your nickname?" Gbagbladza asked.

"I don't have one," I said.

"Nickname no be force. Make we go chop, I dey hung," DJ said.

I followed them to the snack square and bought a bag of plantain chips.

When school closed that day, DJ and Gbagladza walked with me to the roundabout. They were both day students like me. They waited for me to board the hospital bus before they left. I had survived the first day. I had fifty-nine more days to go.

*

"So how was school?" Mama asked when she came home later that night.

"Okay."

"Just okay?"

"Uh huh."

"Did you make friends?"

I thought of all those who had stared at my face. I thought of the girl who had called me Dr Blight and of the other girls who had laughed at me. I thought of how alone I had felt until DJ showed up with his crazy friend, Gbagbladza. "Yes, one."

"That's great," Mama said and I could see she was relieved. "Just give it time, it will all be fine." .

I shook my head, surprised that she didn't have a clue that it would NEVER be fine. "Don't tell me 'it will all be fine', 'cause it won't. I will NEVER be a normal person, not with this face, not when I shit through my stomach!" I went to my room and slammed the door. She didn't come after me.

Later that night both Sofi and Dede called me. We had a conference call.

"How did it go?" Dede asked.

I told them everything including all the bits I had edited out of Mama's version.

"Ignore them," Sofi said and I could feel the anger in her voice. "I'm sure they have inferiority complex issues."

I didn't agree with Sofi but I didn't say anything. How could those girls be feeling inferior? They had everything! They were beautiful, rich, smart and were among the most popular girls in the school.

"Someone will show them one of these days, just you wait and see. What goes around does come around," Dede said.

I immediately felt better. They told me about my old school and old friends but neither of them mentioned Bobby and I didn't ask.

"So are there any cute guys?" Sofi asked.

"Sofi!" Dede shouted.

"What?" Sofi shouted back. "I have nothing against long-distance relationships."

"I don't care about *your* relationships. It was *her* first day. Do you *seriously* think she was checking boys out?"

I smiled as Sofi and Dede continued their bantering. It was just like old times. I missed them so much.

Chapter

6

The rest of the week passed more or less like my first day. Some of the teachers gave us quizzes to find out where we stood. At break time if DJ and Gbabladza did not come for me I remained in the classroom and played my videos of Daddy.

At break time in my second week a girl walked up to me.

"Would you like to join the school choir? We meet once a week, on Fridays, during extracurricular period."

"I can't sing."

"Oh, that's okay. I thought I couldn't sing either till I joined."

"I really can't sing. I go off key and . . ."

She was grinning. "Oh, you're one of those people?"

"Uh huh," I grinned back.

"Aren't you going for break?"

I shook my head.

"Then go and 'throw me'. I want a *bofrot*."

I got up and followed her out of the door. I had noticed her the previous week only because Sefakor had called her 'Alligator'.

Sefakor Deku was the girl who kept calling me Dr Blight. Her sidekicks were Maureen Owusu and Nadya Frimpong.

"I'm Allison Gator, by the way."

"Hi," I said.

Allison was a talker. One of those people who could talk for hours and hours without getting tired. All I had to do was keep saying 'Mmm hmm' or 'Oh' even when I wasn't paying attention.

"What did you sign up for? For extracurricular activity I mean," she asked.

"Ceramics."

"Ceramics? Why do you want to get dirty?"

"I saw some nice pots on the way here. I'd like to learn how to make some."

"Last year I was on the editorial board. This year I'm in the choir."

At the snack square I bought a bag of plantain chips and a sachet of Tampico.

"What's with the plantain chips? It's the only thing you buy when you come here."

I shrugged. "I like chips."

Allison bought two *bofrots* and a bottle of Sprite. We sat down on one of the benches under a gmelina tree.

"Hey, Alligator, when is the next issue of the *Sogasco Filla* coming out?" Sefakor yelled from the opposite side of the snack square.

Allison pretended not to have heard. "I don't think I've hated anyone more in my entire life," she said under her breath.

When Sefakor spotted the captain of the boys' football team, she and her sidekicks went to flirt with him and his teammates.

"Sometimes I wish I could just strangle her."

I followed Allison's gaze to where Sefakor stood with her hand around the captain's waist. He appeared very engrossed in something she was saying or maybe he was just ogling her bust.

"Last year, a group of us approached the school administration and told them we wanted to start a campus magazine. They thought it was a great idea and we started work on it. Sefakor's mother has a printing press in town. We met her and she agreed to print the first issue for us for free. A day to publication, Sefakor came to me and said she wanted to be the feature for the personality profile. We had already interviewed Fafali Dose who was the female sports prefect last year. She had even played for the Black Princesses, the national under seventeen female football team. I told Sefakor it would be impossible to change the story. Mrs Deku called Mari Jata the next day and told her she couldn't print the magazine for us anymore because of 'conflict of interest' issues.

"What conflict of interest issues?"

"Ask again! We had worked so hard to put that edition together. After that Sefakor started calling me Alligator. You know, 'Ally' from Allison and 'Gator'. She knows the right pronunciation of Gator but she prefers to anglicise it. She calls Komi Mensah 'vampire' because of his teeth. In his case, I hate to admit it but, she's on point," she said.

Allison was still talking, "She has a nickname for almost everyone. In class she behaves like an angel so all the teachers like her. On top of all that her father is an MP and an old boy. Her parents donated the water reservoir and built a teacher's bungalow for the school. She's untouchable and she knows it."

I looked over to where Komi Mensah sat by himself eating roasted ripe plantain and groundnuts. He was an outcast, a loner. Though he was in our midst he might as well have been invisible. No one ever noticed him except to tease him about his teeth. He had very prominent canines, but what was worse was that they were not in the same row as his other teeth. They had erupted higher up from his gums and they were the first things you noticed when he spoke, which wasn't often. To be honest they *did* give him a creepy look.

"I don't even know why she's in school. I wish she'd just drop out or something. She's always telling people she's going to stand for Miss Malaika as soon as she turns 18. Last year she won the Miss SHS competition and she was the second runner up in the Mama Hogbe competition."

"What's Mama Hogbe?"

"Miss Hogbetsotso."

*

Allison and I became friends after that. In the mornings she reserved a seat for me at morning assembly then we walked to our classroom together. We paired up also for all our laboratory sessions.

Sefakor started calling us 'Dr Blight and her pet alligator'. We ignored her but that just made her enjoy tormenting us more. In my third week in school all that changed. Sefakor and her friends found a new person to torment.

In the middle of a particularly boring chemistry lecture on redox equations, a boy walked in. A hush descended on the class when he entered. Even the teacher looked surprised to see him. It took me a moment to place him. Like Gbabladza, I never forget a face but unlike Gbabladza I knew where I had met him before. It was the tall boy who had been weeding the plot by our bungalow the day Mama and I had arrived. He had a note in his hand which he gave to the chemistry teacher. The teacher read the note twice before he pointed at the empty seat in front of the class. The boy went over and sat down. As he was getting out his notebook, Sefakor coughed and said, 'murderer'.

The boy, caught off guard, fumbled with his book and dropped it. I expected the teacher to say something. He didn't. He just went back to teaching. I stopped paying attention to what he was saying. What did Sefakor mean by calling him a murderer? Had he really killed someone? If so why wasn't he in prison?

*

At break, the boy was the first out of the classroom. Sefakor, Nadya and Maureen were too busy talking amongst themselves to bother teasing me, Allison or Komi.

The snack square was all abuzz with talk of the new boy.

Gbabladza and DJ Samsizzle walked straight to us when we arrived at the snack square. They had already bought a bag of plantain chips and a sachet of Tampico for me. For Allison they had bought a meat pie and a bottle of Coke.

"Is it true?" Gbabladza asked before we could even sit down.

"Is Jamal Abdullah really back?" DJ asked.

"We heard he was in your class," Gbabladza said.

"Uh huh. I couldn't believe it myself. I thought he was a ghost or something," Allison said.

"Do you guys know him?" I asked.

"Do we know him?" Gbabladza repeated like it was a stupid question.

"He dropped out of school after Form One. If he had stayed, he would have finished school last year. Everyone in the town knows about him," DJ said.

"This is the *filla*," Allison said, getting into her gossipy mode. "He impregnated a girl and then they both dropped out of school. The girl had the baby, but he went to work at one of the spas. Early this year the police found the girl's dead body in floating in the river. She was pregnant and had tried to have an abortion by taking some herbal concoction. They picked him up for questioning but they let him go afterwards. The fishy thing is his co-workers say they don't know where he went during his break on the day the girl died. He insists he was asleep in one of the storerooms."

"Why did they let him go?" I asked.

"They said something, something, insufficient evidence,"

Gbabladza said, "but everyone knows it was his baby."

"You think he gave her the concoction to drink?" I asked.

All three of them looked at me like I had left my brains at home that morning.

"But who else would have given it to her to drink? He was already struggling to take care of the first baby. Do you think he wanted a second one?" Allison asked.

"Everyone knows he killed her," DJ said. "You should have seen Lebene. She was beautiful. As for that one *dea, charley*, don't go there . . ."

"It's true and she wasn't *too known* about her beauty like Sefakor. She was free with everyone. Even her juniors," Allison said.

"But what if . . ." I began saying.

"Look, who else could it have been? A leopard can't change its spots you know?" Gbabladza said. "Besides you weren't here. We knew what he was like when he first moved here. He used to smoke and drink and he belonged to a gang in town."

"Why would he come back if he knows what everyone thinks about him?"

DJ shrugged. He was eyeing the rest of my plantain chips. "Some people have no shame."

I drank the rest of my Tampico. Was there really a murderer in our midst?

"Are you going to eat that?" DJ asked.

I gave him the rest of the plantain chips and he wolfed them down.

With the arrival of Jamal Abdullah things got better for me and Komi Mensah. All attention shifted from us to Jamal Abdullah. If the unsought for attention bothered him, he hid it well. He arrived for class exactly on time each day. I never saw him at the snack square. In class he only spoke when a question was directed at him. I never saw him speak to another student. He didn't contribute to discussions, didn't partake in group work and didn't have a lab partner. If he recognized me, he didn't show that either.

Jamal Abdullah was in my class for exactly one week. The next thing we knew he had been transferred to the visual arts class. I don't know if he couldn't handle the pressure from Sefakor and her cronies or if he really didn't want to study science.

"Good riddance," Sefakor said dramatically that day when he didn't show up. "I mean can you imagine having to breathe the same air with a murderer?"

Maureen and Nadya nodded their heads sympathetically.

"I swear sometimes I felt he was planning something diabolical. He just sat there not talking to anyone from morning till afternoon. It was so creepy."

"Very creepy," Maureen agreed.

"And where does he disappear to at break time? I never see him at the snack square and he wasn't at the library or computer labs either because I checked every single day, the whole of last week," she said.

"Faakor!" Nadya said, her eyes lighting up as she thought

of something. "Maybe he goes to smoke *wee*!"

Sefakor slapped her forehead. "Of course! Why didn't I think of that? He goes to get high at break time. I mean where else would he disappear too?" Sefakor said.

With the exit of Jamal Abdullah from our class, Sefakor's attention turned to me, Allison and Komi Mensah once again.

Chapter 7

"What do you want to be when you grow up?" Allison asked.

We were on our way to our respective extracurricular classes. I'd been following her to her choir rehearsals for three weeks because the ceramics class didn't have a teacher. The teacher who usually taught the class had gone on maternity leave and the substitute teacher had not reported. That morning at assembly, the girls' prefect had announced that those who had signed up for ceramics were to go to the ceramics studio in the visual arts department.

"I don't know yet," I said, kicking a pebble.

"I want to be a journalist. You know, the pen is mightier than the sword kind of thing."

"Cool," I said.

"There are so many things I could be writing about even now, but what's the point if there's no school magazine? Administration said they don't have money for printing it." She adjusted the strap on her school bag and continued walking.

"You can still write," I said.

"How will people read it?"

"Notice boards. You can paste your articles on the SRC notice board. Or you could start a blog on the internet. I have a friend who writes a food and fashion blog."

"Food and fashion? How are those even related?"

I shook my head, "To Sofi, everything is related to food. She writes about new foods she tries and about outfits that catch her attention."

She looked at me for a moment. I could see the wheels in her head turning. Suddenly her face broke into a huge grin. "You're right, I could still write. I like the blog thing. Hey, maybe I'll join the computer people today and ask them about it. See you later, okay?"

"Okay," I said as she changed directions and practically ran to the computer laboratory.

She hadn't gone far when she turned and called, "If it works out, I'll dedicate my first article to you, okay?"

"Okay," I called back.

I went to the girls' washroom to change out of my uniform into my games outfit. Some other girls were also there changing. Just as I was coming out of the last cubicle, Sefakor and her girls walked in and started undressing.

"Hey, see it's Dr Blight. She's going to play with mud."

Sefakor, Maureen and Nadya were in the traditional dance class. Sefakor had told the entire class she was going to dance the *atsiagbekor* during the talent section of the Miss Malaika beauty pageant.

I ignored them and walked out of the washroom. The ceramics class was empty but I could see someone had gone to great lengths to make it look 'homey'. There was a radio in the room (clearly the teacher had not read the rule book), It was tuned in to Joy FM, my favourite radio station. Doreen Andoh was just wrapping up her show, 'Lunch Time Rhythms'. There was a plant growing in a plastic bucket in one corner of the room. I thought that was weird. If they were teaching ceramics, couldn't they at least make a proper flower pot? Pots and other clay objects in various stages of completion lined a shelf on one wall. A stack of old newspapers occupied another shelf. Dried splotches of clay mixture lined the walls and floors. There was another bucket which had a lot of odds and ends—wires, rags, bits of foam, seeds, broken calabashes and gourds, springs and broken clay objects.

There were many poster papers on the walls. Most of them were quotes. Others were organograms on how to make things. I moved around the class reading the quotes:

It is better to do something imperfectly than to do nothing flawlessly. Robert Schuller

Art is a long process which dates from the hidden past, runs through our own modern times and passes into the future. Asihene

Does the clay say to the potter, 'What are you making?' Isaiah 45:9

You gain strength, courage, and confidence by every

experience in which you really stop to look fear in the face. You must do the thing which you think you cannot do. Eleanor Roosevelt

Your life is a piece of clay. Don't let anyone else mould it for you. Unknown

But the pot he was shaping from the clay was marred in his hands; so the potter formed it into another pot, shaping it as seemed best to him. Jeremiah 18:4

Our lives begin to end the day we become silent about the things that matter. Martin Luther King Jnr

The same sun that melts the wax hardens the clay. African proverb

Ceramics to me is a game without rules. It is an endless journey of building and playing. Robert Moore

"Hey, where is everyone?" Gbagbladza asked walking into the class. He threw his bag onto one of the seats and came to stand by my side.

"I don't know. I just got here."

He stood really close to me. "I like this one about doing the thing you fear most."

"They're all really good," I said. "I thought you were taking the web designing programme with DJ."

"I uh . . . I changed my mind," he said. He stepped closer to me. He smelled good. He must have doused himself in perfume after he changed out of his uniform.

"I've been meaning to ask you something."

"Go ahead," I said while hoping he wasn't going to ask

about the accident.

"Well, I . . ."

Just then someone entered the room. She was in a white T-shirt and faded jeans. I hadn't seen her before. I took her to be another new girl like me. She probably hadn't been supplied her games outfit yet. Her hair was cut short like mine but she wore long dangling cowrie earrings and her fingernails were painted a bright yellow. She must not have read the rule book.

"Hi," she said.

"Hi," Gbabladza and I said back.

"You must be new," Gbabladza walked up to her and draped his arm over her neck. "Do you know who is taking us for this class?"

The girl smiled and gently peeled Gbagbladza's arm from her shoulder. "Yes, I *am* new and *I'll* be taking you through the ceramics class. I'm Miss Lartey."

Gbabladza dropped his hand and began stammering, "I'm sor . . . so . . . sorry, Miss, Madam, I didn't know . . ."

Miss Lartey smiled. "It's okay." She looked at me. "Please call the others. They're outside by the kiln."

Jamal Abdullah appeared at the door just as I was about to step out. We did that awkward moving in tandem thing. First we went right together and then we went left together. "Sorry," we both said at the same time. I remained where I was to allow him to pass but he didn't enter the class. I looked up at him with a raised eyebrow.

"Ladies first," he said.

I walked past him to the kiln where I met five other students—two seniors and three juniors. Did Jamal Abdullah think being courteous to me was going to make me forget he was a murderer? When I got back to the pottery studio, Miss Lartey had written her full name on the blackboard: Naa Larteley Lartey. She said we could call her either Naa Larteley or Miss Lartey. I knew for sure she hadn't read the rule book.

"This is the ceramics class," Miss Lartey said when we were all seated.

Duh. Of course it was the ceramics class. What else could it be with a potter's wheel and clay pots on the shelves?

Miss Lartey told us a little about herself. She was a volunteer teacher. She was pursuing an undergraduate programme in industrial arts. She had taken a year off her studies to teach before going back for her final year.

"This will mainly be a practical class. We'll have one theory session but you'll be required to do further reading on your own. I don't want us to get bogged down with too much theory when we come here. The minute you step in this class, nothing else exists. Nothing. It's just you and the clay. There's no past or future. It's the present. Always the present. The first thing you have to understand before we begin working is," she turned and wrote on the board: RESPECT.

I knew it! She wasn't even a *real* teacher yet and she was already behaving like one. I was waiting for her to say how she wouldn't tolerate lateness and noisemaking or any of the other a hundred and one things that teachers have no tolerance for when she said, "You have to respect the clay."

Someone behind me snickered. Even I was confused.

"Yes, respect. Clay has a mind of its own. It shows you what to do and what not to do with it."

She walked around the room and passed out fist sized lumps of clay.

"Respect the clay is the only rule in this class. By the end of the term you should have produced something, anything at all. The only thing I require is that the thing you create should be important to you. You will write an essay of between a hundred to two hundred words explaining why your creation is important to you. Is that understood?"

Though we groaned most of us nodded.

"Good. I am here to show you how to work with the clay; how to get it to do what you want but what you will produce is entirely up to you."

I heard giggling and snickering from the back of the class and turned to look. One of the senior boys had rolled his clay into an erect penis and had placed it on his crotch. He was moaning 'Lebene, Lebene' under his breath. I turned to look at Jamal. He was looking straight ahead, his face expressionless but his jaw hardened and a muscle twitched. By the time Miss Lartey turned to look at what was happening behind her, the boy had rolled the clay back into a lump.

"You must take chances with this lump of clay. You will fail repeatedly but don't let that stop you." She tossed her lump up and down. "This lump is asking you to pursue it, to seek it, to discover what it can be. Never give up on it. If you listen hard enough, you will hear the clay tell you what it wants to be. Anytime you make something with this clay, you're making something unique. Something that has never been made before and will never be made again. No matter how many times you try to reproduce it, you'll never get the exact, same thing. They'll always be duplicates of the original, 'original duplicates' if you like."

I looked at Miss Lartey. Did she even know she had used an oxymoron? 'Original duplicates' was a great oxymoron. Daddy would have loved it. I remembered what Miss Lartey had said about no past and no future and concentrated on the present—the lump of clay in my hand. I wondered what I would make. What was important to me?

"Don't let your frustrations or your past failures drive you. In this room, there is no past, no future. There's only the here and now. Only the present. Only you and this lump. I want you to keep experimenting, keep exploring and keep trying till you get it right."

I squeezed the lump in my hand until clay slipped out between my fingers. I wondered what my lump was telling me.

"Okay, let's get the theory session out of the way so we can go right down to working with the clay next week."

She spent the next thirty minutes giving us a crash course in ceramics. She spoke of how clay was formed from decomposed granite rocks. The granite rocks themselves were formed from the lava of volcanoes and had been exposed to weathering which broke them into smaller pieces. The process took place over millions of years for us to get clay in the form we were holding.

She told us how traditional potters scattered over all parts of Ghana had been able to produce perfectly symmetrical pots without using the potter's wheel. She showed us pictures of women making pots on the ground. She told us of ceramic products and showed us pictures of ceramics produced by other cultures, pointing out the similarities and differences between them.

"If you have time, go to Vume and see how our people make their pots. It's a similar process that's used all over the country. I tried to get the school administration to organise an excursion for us but they say they don't have money. Find time and go yourselves. You'll learn a lot from the potters."

She told us about Michael Cardew, who came to Ghana in 1942 and taught art in Achimota school. It was he who introduced Ghanaian potters to the potter's wheel, kilns and glazes. In 1952, the art department was moved from Achimota to Kumasi and formed part of the Kumasi College of Technology. In 1961 it was renamed as the Kwame Nkrumah University of Science and Technology.

She gave us thick hand-outs and a program outline with topics we were supposed to read before we came for the practical class. I tuned her out when she began talking about kilns and glazes. If I'd known she'd be doing so much talking I wouldn't have come to the class. I would probably have followed Allison to the computer lab. At the end of the class, Miss Lartey told us the ceramics studio would be open throughout the week so we could come in anytime we had a free period to work on our projects.

Gbabladza walked me to the roundabout to wait for the hospital bus. DJ was staying behind to finish something he had begun during the web designing class. Allison had gone for lunch in the dining room with the other boarders.

"Miss Naa is cool," he said.

"Yeah, very cool. I just hope she'll not talk so much next time. What will you make?"

Gbabladza shrugged. "I don't know. I only joined because DJ said you signed up for ceramics."

"Oh," was all I could say.

"Can I ask you what I wanted to ask earlier?"

I nodded.

"So do you like have a boyfriend in Accra?"

"Huh?" Not that I should have been surprised but I was. Gbabladza had started calling me at home and on weekends and sending me funny WhatsApp texts and picture messages. I should have seen it coming.

"Are you going out with anyone?"

It was the first time in the entire week that I had thought of Bobby.

"Yes."

"Oh."

We were both quiet for some time.

"Is it serious?"

"Yes," I lied. *Was it still serious if you were on a break?*

I could see the hospital bus coming towards us. Gbabladza saw it too.

"I just . . . I really like you. If it doesn't work out with the other guy, let me know, okay?"

I nodded and entered the bus the minute it stopped. I didn't turn to look at Gbabladza as the driver drove away. Was he serious? Couldn't he see my face?

Chapter
8

Mama dropped me at Uncle Larweh's house the next day. DJ and I spent most of the morning working quadratic equations. He hadn't been exaggerating when he said he was bad at maths but I didn't mind tutoring him. At lunch time we went to the kitchen for a meal of *akple* and *fetri detsi*. It was a good thing that Mama wasn't there to see all the palm oil floating on the top of the soup. When I saw DJ's ball of *akple* (it was thrice the size of mine) I asked him if he would be able to finish it. He only grinned and said, "With God all things are possible."

I'm not as picky as Mama, so I enjoyed the meal thoroughly. In addition to meat and smoked herrings, Auntie Cee had added oysters, shrimps and crabs to the soup. After helping DJ with the dishes, he volunteered to take me on a tour of the town. We ended up wading in the river because I was terrified of riding behind him on his motorcycle. He didn't even have a helmet. When it got too hot, he took me to a spot where we had some ice cream.

We stayed there until it grew dark but no one asked us to leave. DJ said we were waiting for the kebab guy. He swore that the guy's kebabs were the best in the entire South Tongu district. When I noticed a waiter coming our way, I asked DJ how to say 'Please, where is the washroom?' in Ewe.

DJ told me to say, *"Medekuku me lor wɔ."*

When the waiter approached our table I said, *"Medekuku me lor wɔ."*

"Sorry?" the waiter said.

I turned to look at DJ whose face was expressionless. *"Medekuku me lor wɔ,"* I repeated stupidly thinking there was a problem with my pronunciation.

The waiter looked from me to DJ. Then he looked back at me and then at DJ. It was only then that I saw that DJ was trying very hard not to laugh.

The waiter turned to me, smiled and said, "I love you too but I already have a girlfriend."

It took me a minute to process everything. By then DJ was laughing so hard that he nearly fell off his chair.

My face grew hot. "I'm sorry . . . I didn't mean . . . I had no idea what I was saying . . ."

"Charley long time, how be tins?" DJ asked bumping fists with the waiter.

"We just dey. How we for do am?" the waiter replied.

I couldn't believe they knew each other. I sat there with my mouth hanging open.

"My cuson dis, e no know the Ewe."

"Me naa I see. Why we see you kyεε like so?"

"No be my ol' man? He say my grades no good so, charley, I no fi spin again."

"Yawa o. You for mow the book."

"E no be easy o."

"Nothing be easy. Charley, I have job do, I go see you ron." They bumped fists again. He took our empty bowls and was chuckling when he walked away. I leaned over to hit DJ but he grabbed my hand and started laughing all over again. Then he pointed the way to the washroom and I went to pee. When I came back he was still laughing.

"I'll get you for that. You just wait and see," I said.

"You should have seen the look on your face—it was priceless. I should have taped it."

We were the first to order the goat meat kebabs when the kebab guy came and DJ was right, they were very good. He even let me take the extra stick the guy gave us.

"I used to spin there on weekends," he said as we walked to the *trotro* station. "The manager hasn't got anyone to take my place yet. I'm hoping if I do better this term, Dad will let me go back to spinning."

He bought us some *kelewele* and fried groundnuts while we waited for the taxi that would pass in front of the hospital to finish loading.

"Thanks for teaching me," he said when the last person sat in.

"Thanks for taking me round. I had a good time," I heard myself say and was even more surprised to find out that I meant every word of it.

*

"What are we doing for your birthday?" Mama asked three weeks later as we were driving home from church. The Pastor had preached a sermon on treasures in clay pots. I'd liked it very much.

My birthday was the next day. I had thought Mama had forgotten about it. It was six weeks since we had moved to Sogakofe. Six weeks. I'd been so busy helping Allison out with her blog that I had hardly noticed the time fly. We had spent one weekend making posters and flyers to whip up interest. It had taken her forever to decide on a name. She had thought 'Campus *Filla*' was too dry and 'Eyes and Ears' sounded like a tacky gossip column. She had finally settled on 'Musings of a Sogascan'. It didn't sound bad to me either and so the name stuck. She had so far published two articles. The first was 'What is your cross?' and was dedicated to me like she promised. She was always running to the computer lab to check how many hits she had.

"Do you want to send a cake to school? I could also order food for you and your friends."

"Mom, I'm not in primary school anymore," I said. I could imagine the looks on Sefakor, Maureen and Nadya's faces if my mother appeared on campus with a cake and food. There was no way I'd live down their teasing and taunts.

I turned to Mama with a stricken look on my face, "Please promise that you won't come to school with a cake or food or drinks or anything."

"Hey, okay, okay."

"Promise," I insisted.

"I promise," she said.

"We could go to the spa for the weekend. There are two of them by the river you know? One of them is a health spa."

I groaned.

"It'll be fun, you wait and see."

I sighed. Spending a weekend with my mother eating whole grains, fresh fruits and vegetables and doing 'fun exercises' was not my idea of fun.

*

On my birthday, I wore lip gloss and a put some face powder on my face. I washed it all off when I looked in the mirror. The face powder just drew more attention to the scars. I reapplied the gloss. Rules were made to be broken after all.

My phone beeped. I was reading the WhatsApp message from Dede when it beeped again.

Dede's message read: HBD. May all ur hrts desires come true. Hv a gud day. ttyl, aight?

Sofi's read: May u increase lyk bofrot in H2O ☺ May any evil plans against u go bak 2 sender. May joy n peace n hapiness be urs now & always. Hapi 17 bday. Luv u.

Mama was in a very good mood. She even fried an egg for herself, after she made an egg sandwich for me. She hardly ever eats egg.

"You look pretty. Happy birthday."

"Thanks," I said sitting down to eat.

She disappeared into her bedroom and came back with a box.

"Here you go, happy birthday."

I put down my mug of Milo and opened the box. In it was a simple gold chain with a tiny heart-shaped locket. Inscribed on the locket were the words 'To the one I love'.

"That was the first gift your dad ever gave me."

"I know," I said, caressing the locket. "Thank you." I clasped the chain around my neck and slipped it under my shirt.

"I thought your school had a no jewellery policy."

"No one will see it," I said.

Mama sat down and picked her mug of herbal tea. Out of the blue she said, "The first time I noticed him was in the dissection room in medical school."

I'd heard the story of how they met over a hundred times from Daddy. This was the first time I was hearing it from Mama.

"We knew we were going to be cutting up dead bodies but I guess it never really sunk in till we walked into the dissection room. There were eight cadavers on the dissection tables—two female and six males. We were assigned tables and we stood around them. The head of the anatomy department came in to talk to us about respecting the bodies, about how the people had given themselves to advance the spread of knowledge. He was still speaking when this tall boy, or man I should say started sweating. I saw him wipe his face with a handkerchief and fan his face with his fingers. The next thing I knew he had fallen on top of me."

I giggled. "He said it was love at first sight, when he opened his eyes and saw you."

"He lied," she said chuckling. "They laid him on one of the empty cadaver tables and gave him a bottle of coke to drink. I had to be sent to the sick bay. I had a bump the size of a fist on my head."

She took a forkful of scrambled eggs.

"He felt really bad about it. He came to see me in my room at the hostel that night. Then we began saying 'hi' to each other at lectures. He fainted two more times. Again in the dissection room and another time in the haematology lab when blood was being drawn for an experiment we were doing. The head of the department called him and had a talk with him. Turned out blood made him squeamish and he didn't really want to do medicine; it was what his family wanted. He loved mathematics. He wanted to be a maths teacher. He dropped out of medical school and went to read maths at Legon. We kept in touch. When I graduated I invited him to my party. We started dating, got married and had you."

We finished our breakfast in silence. This was the longest talk we had had about my father. I knew she had done it so I wouldn't feel his absence so much it being my birthday and all. I wanted to tell her I appreciated the gesture; that I was glad she had made us talk about him but I didn't. She got up, rinsed out her mug and plate and the moment passed.

*

At break that day I told Allison that I wasn't feeling well. She went for break alone. I wanted to play a video of Daddy but Komi Mensah also hadn't gone for break and I didn't know if he would report me if he saw me with a phone.

I remembered what Miss Naa had said about keeping the ceramics studio open and went there instead. I sat at one of the corners at the back and played the video of Daddy dancing to Kojo Antwi's Tom and Jerry *awareε*. I don't know where the tears came from but they started pouring down my face.

"Hey, are you okay?"

I was so scared that I dropped the phone. I hadn't heard Jamal Abdullah enter the classroom. He picked up the phone, glanced at the screen for a moment and gave it back to me. I fumbled with the off button.

"Are you okay?" he repeated.

I wiped the tears off my face.

"Stupid question, obviously, you're not okay. Should I call someone for you? Allison? DJ?"

I shook my head.

He sat down at the desk next to mine.

"Are you going to report me?" I asked when I found my voice.

"For what? For crying?"

"The phone."

"Of course not. That's an irrational rule. I wonder what made Mari Jata come up with that one."

I didn't know what else to say.

"Do you mind if I stay? I want to practise on the wheel."

I shook my head.

"Are you sure? I mean if you want to be alone, I can come back another time."

"It's okay," I said.

He walked up to the corner of the room where some balls of clay had been kept in a plastic bowl and covered with a plastic sheet. He picked up a ball and kneaded it on a slab the way Miss Naa had taught us to do. In no time at all his hands were muddy. He took the piece of clay, sat behind the potter's wheel and placed the ball on the wheel. I think he forgot I was in the room. He had really taken Miss Naa's words to heart. It was just him and the clay.

The ball of clay wobbled on the wheel. He took it off the wheel and slapped it down again. Then he leaned forward and cupped it with his hands. His forearms remained firmly planted on his thighs. His eyebrows furrowed in concentration. He wet his hands in a bowl of water at his side and forced the clay down. Then he cupped it with both hands and forced it up. He forced it down again and made a hole in the centre with his thumb. I don't know how he managed to pedal with his foot and work with his hands at the same time.

When he was satisfied with the size of the hole he placed both hands into the opening and opened it up further. The next stage happened like magic. He kept one hand in the pot and the other on the outside, and the pot just began growing. I really don't know what he did next, the wheel was spinning really fast and his hands were all over the place, but I could see a vase take shape. It had a well-rounded base, a tubular neck and a flared mouth for the opening.

"Wow," I said.

I must have startled him because his hand slipped and one wall of the vase fell in. He looked up and seemed surprised to see me. He stopped pedalling and the wheel ground to a stop.

"Sorry, I didn't mean to startle you."

"It's okay. I was almost done anyway," he said and crushed the rest of the clay.

"I thought everyone in the class was a beginner." In our extracurricular class, we were still struggling with pinching the clay to get something which would pass for a pot. No matter how hard I tried I couldn't get the walls to be even. When Miss Naa had demonstrated it had looked so easy.

He shrugged. "I've worked with clay before."

I wondered if that was before he'd dropped out of school. He must have guessed what I was thinking because he frowned and turned away from me. He took the lump of clay back to the bucket in the corner and washed his hands. Then he picked up his bag and left.

"Jamal wait," I called after him. It had occurred to me that this was where he had been coming all along. He hadn't been going to smoke *wee* or anything of that sort. He stopped, turned and raised an eyebrow in question.

"Can I come and watch you tomorrow?"

"No," he said and walked away.

*

The next day at break time Allison said she had to update her blog. I didn't know what I would do if DJ also decided not to show up. Things had become awkward between Gbabladza and me. I rushed to the ceramics studio and was out of breath when I got there.

Jamal was already behind the potter's wheel. He was centring the ball of clay (the previous night I had speed-read all the hand-outs Miss Naa had given us and had been pleased to recognise the steps Jamal had been practising on the wheel).

I walked into the studio. Jamal scowled when he saw me.

"I said I didn't want you here."

"Miss Naa said the studio was open to *anyone* to come and practise," I said and went to the bin. I picked a ball of clay of my own. I kneaded it the way Miss Naa had taught us to and sat behind one of the desks. I cupped the lump of clay in my left hand, stuck my right thumb down the middle of the clay and spied Jamal out the corner of my eye. He was pulling up the walls of the pot. He must have done something wrong because a piece of the clay just came off in his hand.

"Drat!" he mumbled.

I went back to what I was doing and continued watching Jamal as he crushed the lump of clay and began the process all over again. This time he managed to successfully pull the walls of the pot. My left hand had begun to stiffen and hurt from cupping the ball of clay for so long. I wondered if it would ever heal. I dropped the ball back into the bucket and went to my classroom to pump my rubber ball.

*

The next day Allison disappeared at break time to check the number of hits she had had and to read people's comments. The day before she had had sixty-three hits and twenty seven Facebook likes for her article.

I ran to the ceramics studio and was disappointed to find that Jamal wasn't there. I waited for ten minutes, but he didn't show up. I was about to go to the snack square when I remembered Allison wouldn't be there. I didn't like the thought of running into Gbabladza so I decided to practise my own modelling. I picked up a ball of clay, kneaded it, stuck my thumb into its centre and alternated between pressing my thumb against the wall and rotating the ball of the clay. Press, rotate. Press, rotate. Press, rotate. I was so caught up in what I was doing that I was startled when Jamal spoke.

"You should work from the base up now."

He was seated on a desk by the door. I don't know how long he had been there or how long he had been watching me.

"Huh?"

"You should start pulling, by working from the base up."

I was thrilled that he had spoken to me using a technical term and that I had understood it. I began pulling. He kept watching me, but I soon forgot him. It was just me and the clay but I must have pulled too much because a gap appeared in one of the walls.

I sighed and put the pot down.

Jamal got up, went to one of the shelves, picked something

up and came to my desk. He had a cup in his hand. In it was a mix of clay and water called 'slurry'. He picked up my pot; I noticed that he was left-handed. He dipped a finger into the slurry and pinched the clay back into place.

"It's clay. Any mistake you make is fixable." He placed my pot back on the table, washed his hands and left.

For the rest of the week, I spent all my break periods in the ceramics studio. Allison didn't notice. She and DJ were designing a web page for an online students' newspaper and they used every free period they had to work at the computer lab. Jamal didn't scowl at me anymore. Sometimes he helped me with my modelling. Other times he completely ignored me.

In our next extracurricular class, Miss Naa remarked on how well my pinched pots had improved. I soaked up the praise but not before I had seen Jamal try unsuccessfully to hide a smile.

Chapter

9

After school that Friday, Mama was waiting for me at the roundabout. I spotted her car and noticed there were two people in the back seat. Had the hospital bus broken down? Why was she picking up staff? When I got closer, the back door opened and Sofi and Dede jumped out.

"Surprise!"

"Happy belated birthday!"

Before I could react they were both hugging me and talking non-stop.

"Your mother called our parents last week to ask if we could spend the weekend together. Can you believe it?" Dede asked. She was in blue jeans, a black T-shirt and black sandals.

"It was so hard speaking to you and trying to act natural when we knew we'd be seeing you this weekend," Sofi gushed. She was in purple tights, a yellow mini-skirt, an orange and blue frilly blouse and green ballet flats that had pink bows on top. Stuck in her hair were blue sunglasses. A stack of multi-coloured bangles were on one arm and dangling seashell earrings were on her ears.

In some part of my mind 'act natural' registered but I was much too happy to dwell on it.

"Girls, I have to get back to work," Mama called from the car.

I followed Sofi and Dede to the car. All three of us crammed into the backseat. The girls wouldn't let me talk.

"We got here like ten minutes ago and your mother came for us at the station," Dede said.

Sofi was unwrapping fried yam and *chofi* which I was sure she had bought after the toll booth.

"It's getting cold," she said when she caught Dede looking at her. She bit into the *chofi* and said, "Mmm, it's so good."

"And that matters how? I thought you said you bought it to take pictures for your blog," Dede said.

Sofi picked up another slice of fried yam and said, "We wanted to come to your school but your mother said we should wait at the roundabout."

I picked a slice of the yam and nibbled. I couldn't believe they were really there. It was so good to see them.

"It took you forever to get here. *Ah ah*, what were you doing? Did you have games or something? Were you playing football? You have mud on your shirt," Sofi said.

I was still in my games outfit. I looked down at my shirt. There were dried spots of slurry splattered across it.

"It's clay," I said scraping off a spot with a fingernail. "I take ceramics for extracurricular activity."

"You're not in the science and maths club?" Dede asked.

"No."

"Why?"

I shrugged. "No reason." I didn't want to talk about how it would only remind me of Daddy. Not with Mama within hearing distance. I looked out the window and was surprised to see we were nowhere near the hospital. Mama was pulling up in the parking lot of the spa. Thankfully, it wasn't the health spa.

"Mama?"

She looked at me in the rear-view mirror and smiled. "Your bag is in the boot."

We got down and she went with us to the reception where she had made reservations for us. I carried the shoulder bag Mama had packed my things into. Dede picked up her small travelling bag. Sofi struggled with her two suitcases.

"Uh, how long are you staying?" I asked.

"Ever heard of travelling light?" Dede asked.

She dragged her suitcases and stopped to rest after every two steps before saying, "I like to travel in style and comfort."

"I'll pick you up Sunday at noon, okay?" Mama said.

I nodded. A lump had begun forming in throat.

Mama hugged me and whispered, "Happy birthday." I followed her back to the car.

"But, Mama, the cost?"

"Don't worry about it. Have fun. Pamper yourself. You only get to be seventeen once."

"Thanks," I said.

"No, *thank you*. I know adjusting to life here isn't easy for you and though you insist that school is 'okay' I know it isn't. This weekend, I want you to forget about everything and just have fun with your friends. Okay?"

"Okay."

She hugged me once more and left.

"I'm starving," Sofi said when I went back to the reception. "Let's eat."

"Let's see our room first," Dede suggested. She had the key to our room in her hand.

"Yes, let's. Besides I have to change."

Our room was located in another building on the opposite side of the compound. The walk gave us a chance to take in our surroundings. The environment was quiet and peaceful and there was so much greenery in sight. A water fountain stood in the centre of the compound. There were geese and peacocks everywhere. We stood for a minute waiting to see if a peacock would spread out its feathers, but it didn't. We did find some feathers that had been shed on the grass and we picked two each. Just being in that environment made me relax. Our room had a twin bed and a beautiful view of the river. Dede opened her travelling bag and began to put away her clothes while I changed my clothes and colostomy bag in the bathroom. Sofi plopped down on the bed, unwrapped the complimentary bar of Golden Tree chocolate that had been left on the nightstand and began to eat it.

When I finished all three of us went to the restaurant which was located on a platform on the river. Since it was past lunch time there were just two other couples there. Dede said the first couple were on their honeymoon. Their heads were close together and they kept whispering and giggling as they sipped their drinks and waited for their food.

The second couple were older. They sat on opposite sides of the table and ate their *fufu* with *akponkye nkrakra* without talking. The woman looked angry. The man looked like he didn't know what they were doing there. I said they were business partners who were having a disagreement. Dede said they were a married couple who were trying to put the spark back into the marriage, giving their marriage one last shot before deciding to end it.

Sofi didn't have an opinion. She was busy looking through the menu and trying to decide what to eat. Our waiter appeared and we ordered our food and drinks. He brought the drinks first. Dede and I both had Alvaros. Mine was passion fruit flavoured. Dede's was pear flavoured. Sofi had a bottle of malt.

Dede was showing me pictures on her phone when Sofi said, "He's cute."

I turned to look at who she was talking about and nearly choked on the Alvaro I had in my mouth. The drink came out of my mouth and nose. Tears appeared in my eyes. I began coughing and more drink splattered the table. Dede thumped my back. Sofi put a glass of water in front of me and used a tissue to wipe the table.

My coughing fit drew the attention of the waiter who was

serving the honeymooners. The same waiter who Sofi had said was cute—Jamal Abdallah. He was in a starched white shirt and black trousers. He seemed as surprised to see me as I was to see him. After he had put the plates of food down he started walking over to where we sat.

I raised a hand to stop him. "I'm fine," I sputtered.

He raised an eyebrow.

"Truly, I'm fine."

He nodded and walked away.

"What was that all about?" Sofi asked when he was out of earshot.

"What was what all about?"

"I mean you looked at the guy and started choking and then you guys had some like telepathic thingy going on. Dee didn't you notice it?"

"Very telepathic thingy," Dede confirmed.

I rolled my eyes.

"So?" Sofi persisted.

"So nothing. He's just a boy from school. I was surprised to see him here, that's all."

"Hmm," Dede said her face breaking into a grin.

"I thought *you* said there were no cute boys in your school," Sofi said.

"I didn't . . ."

"Wait, wait, wait," she raised her hand interrupting me. "Dee, remember her first day of school?"

"Uh huh."

"Remember how *I* asked if there were *any* cute boys in her school?"

"Uh huh."

"And what was her answer?"

"I don't think she gave you one."

"Hey, the only reason I couldn't . . ."

Sofi's hand shot up, silencing me. She continued as if she hadn't heard me. "My point exactly! She evaded the question which, if you think about it logically, could only mean two things!"

"Two things," Dede agreed.

"That number one," she ticked it off on her finger, "there were cute boys in her school *and* number two, that she liked one of them."

I groaned and rested my head on my hands. "How did you even come up with that?"

"Logical reasoning," she said smiling at me sweetly and taking a gulp of her malt. "Now tell us *everything*."

Our waiter brought our food—*jollof* rice and grilled tilapia for Dede, shrimp fried rice and grilled tilapia for Sofi, and French fries and roast chicken for me. Over our meal I told them what I knew about Jamal. I'm not exactly sure why but I left out the part about him having been a murder suspect. I also left out the fact that I had seen him every day at the ceramics studio the past week.

*

The next day we went for a cruise on the Volta River. Our tour guide was a grumpy old man and he didn't really say much. It was supposed to be an hour's cruise but after thirty minutes we asked him to take us back to the spa. All three of us decided to get facial treatments. We each had to change into a towel. We even had to wrap our heads in another towel.

The facial room itself was relaxing. There were lots of potted plants and bright sunlight streamed in through the many windows. Instrumental music played softly in the background. We each entered a different cubicle. The lady who did my facial was a real professional and she told me what she was doing each step of the way. She didn't make me feel self-conscious about my scars.

She began by rubbing with my face with cotton wool soaked in some lotion. She sprayed steam on my face and afterwards applied a green gooey paste to my face. She told me it was a mix of clay, cactus and aloe vera. She even put two round slices of cucumbers on my eyes just like in the movies. The mask remained on my face till it hardened. She said it would draw impurities out of my body. While the mask hardened she massaged my scalp. It felt really good and I drifted off to sleep. When I woke up she had washed the mask off. I felt wonderful. I felt like I was glowing and like my entire face was 'breathing'.

The girls and I had lunch on the restaurant by the river. This time all three of us ordered *banku* with grilled tilapia. It came with three different types of pepper. There was the *kpakpo shitɔ*, the regular smoked herring and shrimp *shitɔ,* and tomato and red pepper *shitɔ*. There was a side dish of sliced tomatoes, onions and avocados. We had fresh coconut water straight from the trees by the river. After lunch, we stretched out on chairs by the riverside.

"Your mom is so cool," Dede said.

"She's amazing. This is like paradise," Sofi agreed.

I realized how thoughtful it was of Mama to invite Sofi and Dede over. I took out my phone and sent her a text: We r havng a fabulous tyme. Dis is da gr8st b'day ever. Thx. C u 2moro.

I lay back and enjoyed the warmth of the sun on my body. It was too hot to do anything. It was even too hot to wade in the river. Dede and Sofi both dozed off. I got up reluctantly and went back to the room to empty my colostomy bag.

I was still in the bathroom when Dede walked in. I was about to call her when I realized she was on the phone. I could see her through the partially open door. She took the phone from her ear and put it on the bed. It was now on speakerphone. She picked up a pair of shorts from the wardrobe and started unbuttoning her jeans.

The person she was speaking to said, "Yes, I knew her birthday was on Monday."

I froze. It was Bobby.

"So why didn't you call her?"

"We're on a break?"

"A break? What for? Why?" Dede asked, hopping on one foot as she removed her jeans.

"Ask her to tell you."

"I'm asking you to tell me."

"Look, we both have different priorities right now and I can't afford to be distracted. I can't handle any of her emotional problems."

"Oh Bobby!"

"I'm sorry but that's the way it is."

"It's not too late. You can still call her. Tell her you forgot or something. It would mean a lot to her."

"I didn't forget. Why should I lie? She understands we're on a break."

"What's wrong with you? She . . ."

"Look, I don't mean to be rude but I have to go. Bye."

The phone beeped signalling that the connection had been cut. "Idiot," Dede muttered under her breath. She picked up her shorts and marched straight to the bathroom. She jumped when she saw me.

"You've been here all along."

I nodded.

"You heard everything."

I nodded again. I sat on the edge of the bathtub while Dede peed.

"You actually agreed to this 'break' thing? Sometimes I think you have some type of self-destructive disorder."

"I didn't really have a choice."

She stood up, flushed and washed her hands. "You *always* have a choice."

"You can't force someone to love you," I said.

"So why are you still going on with this . . . this . . . this . . ."

"Non-rational arrangement?"

"Exactly."

"I don't know. I guess I'm hoping that maybe by the end of the term he'll realize he likes me and that I'm still the same person, even though I have scars."

Dede put on her shorts and zipped them up. "If he doesn't realize that you're still you, maybe he isn't worth hanging on to."

I looked at her with a grief-stricken look on my face.

"I mean do you really, really in your heart of hearts really, really love him?"

"Of course I do."

"I know you've had this crush on him since Form One but I wonder if he feels the same way about you?"

"What do you mean?" I asked, with a sinking feeling in my stomach.

"It's the little things that he does. You know like when we're together all he does is talk about himself and how he's going to do this or that or something else. Sometimes I think *you* are just with him because you're grateful he chose you to be his girlfriend. And most times I think *he* chose you only to get your Dad to notice him so he could be on the next maths and science team."

I just stared at her. Each word pierced my heart like a dagger. It wouldn't have hurt so much if I hadn't known she was speaking the truth.

"I mean seriously, I'm telling you this because you're my friend, my best friend. If Bobby doesn't know the scars you have aren't your fault, do you think you should be with him? I'd hate for you to be with someone not because you love them, but because you feel grateful to them. That's so not right."

I looked down at the marble floor. I could feel tears pricking the back of my eyes.

She gave me her phone. "You know he's going to dump you at the end of the term. Don't wait for him to dump you. Dump him first. I promise you'll feel much better afterwards."

"He won't. He just wants to sort himself out. He loves me."

Dede stopped short of rolling her eyes. "Okay, let's try something. Call him and tell him you want to break up. If there's any chance he still loves you, he'll try to talk you out of it."

I stared at the phone for a long time because I knew what Dede had said was reasonable. I picked it up and watched my fingers as they punched in Bobby's number. They seemed to know which buttons to push by themselves.

He picked up on the first ring. "Dede, stop bothering me! Nothing you can say will change my mind. I'm not calling her!"

"Bobby, it's me," I said swallowing the lump in my throat.

"Uh hi, I didn't . . ."

"I want us to break up," I said before I lost my nerve.

"Why?" he asked and I felt hope soar in me like a bird in flight. 'Why?' meant he still cared.

"You were right. We have different priorities. There'd be no point in carrying on a relationship."

He was silent for a moment and then he said, "I'm so glad you feel this way. I wanted to tell you the day you were moving but you kept going on and on about being happy to see me that I . . . ."

The flying bird fell to the ground, dead. "I have to go now. Bye," I hung up on him as tears flowed down my face.

"Do you need a hug?" Dede asked.

I didn't trust myself to speak. I nodded. Dede enfolded me in an embrace and I cried my heart out.

Sofi rushed in saying, "You'll never guess . . . ." she stopped when she saw me crying. "What's going on?"

"She just broke up with Bobby."

"Aww, these long distance things . . ." she said and hugged me too.

When I had dried my tears, Sofi remembered the news she had been ready to spill.

"Supper tonight is going to be only continental food. One of the waiters said there'll be a live band so we can dress up if we want!"

"But we didn't bring anything dressy," Dede said.

"Speak for yourself," Sofi said leading the way to one of her suitcases. She opened it to reveal clothes, clothes and more clothes. "Lucky for you I travel in comfort and style," she said with a smug look on her face.

*

Supper indeed was a grand affair and by then I wasn't as depressed as I thought I'd be over the break up. Maybe some part of me had known all along that Bobby and I would break up. Maybe I had even begun preparing myself for it and now that it had happened I wasn't as hurt as I should have been.

Sofi was in her element. She made up my face and painted my fingernails hot pink (though I told her I'd have to clean the polish off before Monday). I drew the line though when she gave me a long, bright, yellow sheath dress. I didn't want to look like a banana. Instead I settled for a short black dress which had elbow length lace sleeves. She looked disappointed but she brightened and said, "Black is always chic."

She pulled out a green, red and blue dress for Dede. Dede shook her head and said, "Don't even go there." Dede wore blue skinny jeans and a purple blouse.

Sofi looked like a peacock when she finished dressing. Her outfit was in all the colours of a rainbow. I couldn't really tell what she was wearing. It looked like a cross between a sarong and a smock and it had long billowing sleeves that came almost to her fingernails. She paired her attire with five inch green stilettos. Dede wore the sandals she had brought. I wore the black ballet flats I had worn to school on Friday.

"One for Facebook," Sofi said making the peace sign and taking a picture of herself. We each posed and took pictures— singles, doubles and then all three of us on Sofi's Samsung Galaxy tab.

*

Tables and chairs had been arranged around the fountain for supper. Thousands of twinkling lights sparkled in the foliage. It looked like we had stepped into some enchanted land. The band had set up near the reception. It turned out that none of the other guests had packed dinner clothes either. Sofi and I stood out like baobab trees in the savannah, but Sofi said to anyone who looked our way, "It's her birthday!" so complete strangers came up to me and wished me "A very happy birthday."

The elders of some churches had who had come for a retreat felt compelled to pray for me and I let them. The head waiter led us to the seat of honour which was by the fountain.

"I'm not eating anything, I can't pronounce," Dede said.

"You have no sense of adventure," Sofi said. "I think I'll order something light. I'm still full from the *banku*."

A waiter came and we placed our orders. I looked around to see if Jamal was on duty. He was busy on another side of the compound. Our eyes met once and I waved. He gave a curt nod in my direction.

"*O la la*," Sofi said when she noticed. I ignored her.

Dede's food came first. She had ordered beef and mushroom stroganoff which turned out to be beef and mushrooms in a very creamy sauce but it tasted good. It came with a side of dish of plain rice and vegetables. I had ordered prawn, chicken and pea paella. I had had no idea what it was. It turned out to be a dish much like *jollof* rice cooked with prawns, chicken and peas. Sofi took pictures with her Galaxy tab and wrote down comments.

"This is good," Sofi said as she took a fourth spoonful of my food.

Dede and I were halfway through our meal before the waiter brought Sofi's food.

"What is this?" she asked when the waiter put her bowl in front of her.

"It's what you ordered."

"I know what I ordered but what is in it?" Sofi asked looking into the bowl in front of her.

"It's *soupe à l'oignon.*"

"Which is what in English?"

I giggled. She should have paid attention in French class.

"Onion soup," the waiter said.

Sofi's *soupe à l'oignon* looked like noodles floating in light soup. There was a slice of bread suspended on top of the soup. Sitting on the top of the bread was a piece of cheese which had begun melting. She didn't know whether to use a spoon or a fork to drink the soup. The noodles kept slipping off the spoon. She gave up on the soup and joined Dede and I to finish our meals.

We hadn't even finished eating when our waiter brought three slices of cake and the band began playing 'Happy birthday to you'. The waiter said the cake was on the house. After supper, Sofi joined a group of people to dance in front of the band. Dede and I watched her. I kept a look out for Jamal, but he didn't look in my direction again.

Chapter

10

Bang. Bang. Bang. The door to the cubicle I was changing in shook.

"I want to use the stall, come out now!"

Sefakor was like a recurring nightmare. I didn't know what to do with her anymore. I changed out of my uniform. I always chose the last cubicle to change in because people hardly ever used it.

Bang. Bang. Bang.

"Why can't you change out here in the aisle like the rest of us? Why do you always lock yourself in that stall? Is your bra stuffed with tissue paper or what?"

When I first arrived in Sogakofe, I had thought my cross was my scarred face. Now I realized it wasn't. People hardly ever stared at me anymore; not even in the main town. My cross was a living breathing talking human being. My cross was Sefakor Deku. The door continued rattling.

I ignored it and finished changing and then I swung the

door open. Sefakor had been about to knock on the door. Her hand landed in the empty air, she lost her balance and went sprawling onto the floor.

"Why don't you get a life and leave other people alone?" I asked as she lay down on the washroom floor.

She just opened and closed her mouth like a fish out of water. Allison and I gathered our things and went for P.E. Maybe things would have ended there and Sefakor wouldn't have got even if Allison hadn't written about it in her blog the next day.

The next morning by break time, Allison's article 'Rumble in the Girls' Washroom' had had over 900 hits and over 700 Facebook likes. In the comment section people dissed Sefakor and called her names and praised me for standing up to her. By the end of the day the hits were almost 1000. By lunchtime the next day, the hits were 1,300 and the likes had climbed to a 1,000. People started smiling and waving at me. I heard someone say, "That's the 'Get a life girl'."

Sefakor and her friends stopped teasing me and Allison. They went their way and we went ours. Allison could hardly keep still in class. She never went for break anymore which was fine by me since I didn't go either. I was always in the ceramics studio and it wasn't just to see Jamal work on the wheel. Miss Naa had taught us how to use ropes of clay to make pots and I was busy practising that.

I had decided what I was going to make for Miss Naa's class. A perfect pot. My essay would be about crosses and crowns and how practising something continuously would eventually produce the result you desire. In my case, my continuous practise sessions were sure to make me end up with the perfect pot.

By break time on Friday, Allison had over 1,800 hits and 1,500 Facebook likes. For a school population of 2,000, that was really something. People had begun waiting for her after class to suggest topics for her to write on. She had become something of a celebrity.

Just before extracurricular class, I received a note from Mr Budu-Smith, our maths teacher, asking me to meet him in the staff common room. As I made my way there I wondered if he had read Allison's blog. I wondered if I was in trouble.

"Hi, Yayra, have a seat."

I sat down on the edge of the seat, all my defences were up. When teachers who have previously not noticed you suddenly take an interest in you, you have to tread cautiously.

"I've been going through your school work and I must say your grades are remarkable. At least they are in maths. I don't know about the other subjects."

I relaxed. Maths was a safe topic. I remembered the school rules so I smiled.

"You are *the* Yayra Amenyo, aren't you?"

I had a blank look on my face. What did he want?

"You are the one who took part in the National Maths and Science Quiz two years ago, aren't you?"

I nodded.

"I knew it! Your team beat Sogasco in the quarter finals

stage, don't you remember?"

I shook my head.

"Well you did." With that proclamation he folded his hands across his chest and looked at me. I didn't know if he expected me to apologise or not. I stiffened.

"Would you like to join this year's team?"

I shook my head again.

"That year's team was our best team. I've been teaching here for fifteen years and that team was the best. This year's is good. They are strong in physics, chemistry and biology but their maths is not as good."

I sat there and watched him, the fake smile fixed on my face.

"We've never even qualified for the semi-final stage. The most we've done is the quarter final where you knocked us out. I'm not trying to pressure you or anything but you would be a wonderful addition to the team. You are exactly what we need."

The blank look was back on my face. I forgot to smile.

"Please think about it carefully and let me have your answer by the end of the month."

I thought I had already given him my answer.

"That will be all now. You may go."

I left the staff common room and ran all the way to the girls' washroom. Mr Budu-Smith had taken twenty minutes out of my ceramics time. I hoped Miss Naa hadn't taught the class any new techniques. The girls' washroom was empty. I ran to the last stall and took off my clothes. I was in so much of a hurry that I didn't notice the latch on the door had not shut properly. Someone had stuck a wad of chewing gum into the hole for the latch.

I had just taken off my shirt when the cubicle door was flung open. Sefakor Deku stood there with Maureen Owusu and Nadya Frimpong. Sefakor grabbed my uniform, which I had hung over the door and Nadya grabbed my bag which had my games outfit in it. I turned away from them. My cheeks were burning and my heart started to pound really hard. I was only in my bra and underwear. Mama was always bugging me about throwing away underwear that was old or that had holes in them. I was glad I'd listened to her. It would have been more humiliating to stand before Sefakor and her friends in torn underwear.

"Turn and look at me," Sefakor ordered.

I ignored her.

"Faakor, we've got what we came for. Let's go, someone will come," Maureen whined.

"You can leave if you want to," Sefakor said to Maureen.

"I said turn and look at me when I'm talking to you," Sefakor said to me. Her voice had a nasty edge to it.

"Do you have leprosy or what? Why all those scars on your arms and back?" Nadya asked.

Sefakor stepped closer to look and noticed my chain. I still had my back to them. "Oh my goodness, you're wearing a chain! Is that what you've been hiding? You're so going to get into trouble when I report you."

I prayed she would leave. I prayed they would all just leave. Even having them see my scarred body was better than having her see me with my colostomy bag.

She walked into the stall and yanked me out of it. She was stronger than she looked. I stumbled out of the stall and fell against one of the sinks. The colostomy bag ripped open. Poop poured out. I wished the floor would open up and swallow me. I felt like the time I had been first diagnosed with inflammatory bowel disease in JHS Two. I had been placed on medication which had seemed to be working until a particular day in school. We had been studying pre-technical skills. I had asked for permission to use the washroom four times in twenty minutes. The fifth time, the teacher thought I was up to something and refused. I didn't make it back to my seat before my bowels spilled open. I had thought the humiliation I felt that day was bad. But this was worse. This was a hundred times worse. No scrap that, this was a million times worse.

Nadya was the first to see my stoma. She screamed, dropped my bag and ran out of the washroom.

Sefakor and Maureen turned to look. I saw the look of horror that passed over their faces. Maureen took a step backwards. A cunning smile passed over Sefakor's face.

"So that's what you've been hiding, eh? What type of *disease* do you have? You've been walking among us like you're normal yet you have a *disease*."

I stood up and picked my bag from the floor.

"I said look at me when I'm talking to you," she yelled.

I dropped the bag, turned, balled my fist and hit her across her face. Sefakor was stunned. I took advantage of that and hit her again. She recovered fast and gave me a slap of her own. In no time at all both of us were on the floor, hitting and punching and smeared in my poop.

Maureen ran to get a teacher. The long and short of it was I didn't make it to extracurricular class that day. After the senior housemistress separated us and we cleaned ourselves up, we got sent straight to the headmistresses' office. We had broken one of the cardinal rules in the rulebook—the no fighting rule. In addition to that I had worn un-prescribed jewellery to school and Sefakor had painted her nails with clear nail polish. Our punishment was a two week internal suspension *with* manual work. The headmistress called both our parents.

Mama arrived first. She had a closed door meeting with the headmistress. Afterwards she took me to the hospital emergency room. I had a split lip. She sutured it for me herself. The lidocaine made my lip feel like it was three times its size, but the pain disappeared immediately. I didn't feel a thing as she sutured. She didn't say a word as she worked. When something happens and Mama is quiet it's very unsettling. I prefer it when she rants and raves. I knew a storm was brewing. Her quietness was the calm before the storm. It might take a week, maybe two before she exploded but when she did it would be nasty.

At home, she asked me to hand over my laptop, my phone and my iPod. I gave them to her without a word. I wished she would ask me what had happened; why I had been in a fight. She didn't. There was no point in trying to explain what had happened. She wouldn't have listened anyway.

*

The next Monday, I knew things had changed. Not only did people know I had fought with Sefakor, people also knew I had a bag on my abdomen which collected my faeces. I was no more the girl who had told off the bully. I was the girl with the *disease*. People didn't know why I was wearing a bag. No one asked. Not even Allison nor DJ. Gbabladza looked relieved that I hadn't agreed to be his girlfriend.

I sat at the back at morning assembly. I was the only one on my bench. People avoided me like the colostomy was catching. After assembly I reported at Mr Amedoda's office. He took Sefakor and I to the school field.

"Weed from here up to that neem tree," he said to me.

That neem tree might as well have been on another planet. The area he had allocated each of us must have been about a third of a football field. The grass came almost up to my waist. I was scared there might be snakes in it.

Sefakor began to protest, "Can't you make me pay a fine or something? I've never weeded before."

"Obey before complain," Mr Amedoda said and left us.

The grass was proper stubborn grass. When you whacked it with the cutlass it just sprang right back up. Big black ants emerged from the ground each time I struck the ground and I spent most of the time stomping my feet so they would not enter my shoes. By the end of the first day, I hadn't done much but my hands were covered in welts. Muscles I didn't know existed in my back and thighs all hurt. I had to stand up in slow motion to not make the pain worse.

Mama was still not talking to me when I got home. I stayed out of her way and she stayed out of mine. I missed my father more than ever. I cried myself to sleep each night. I woke up each morning to Mama doing her aerobics on TV. Whatever closeness had developed between us during my birthday had disappeared.

*

By my third day on the field, I knew that even if I was given two months, I wouldn't finish weeding the plot. I had even brought a pair of scissors from home, but the grass just wouldn't cut. I didn't know how Sefakor was faring since she was on the opposite side of the field. We had steadily avoided each other.

At break time on my third day, I was sitting under the neem tree taking a break when Jamal appeared. I hadn't seen him since the news broke about my stoma. He had a polythene bag in his hand. He came to where I sat and offered me a small Voltic bottle of cold water.

I drank it thirstily. My throat was parched. I finished the entire bottle before I took the bottle from my lips.

"Thanks."

He nodded and opened the bag. "Cutlasses don't work on this grass. This will cut it faster." He brought out a *langa-langa*. I had seen one before but hadn't thought it was any good. He bent down and demonstrated. The *langa-langa* went through the grass like a hot knife through margarine. Cut blades of grass went flying through the air and fell at our feet.

"Thanks," I said.

He shrugged and walked away.

Well-equipped with my new cutting tool, I began working. It wasn't as easy as Jamal made it look, but I could see I was making progress. Jamal took to passing by each day during break time. He didn't come too close to me though; he just stood by the edge of the field. Sometimes he waved and watched me work; sometimes he just stood there and ignored me. Maureen and Nadya passed by each day to see Sefakor but they never stopped to talk to me. Neither Allison, DJ or Gbabladza ever passed by.

Chapter
11

There were two post-it notes stuck to the fridge when I woke up on Saturday. Both were in Mama's handwriting. The first said DJ had called to say he wasn't feeling well and that I wasn't to come over. I knew he was lying. It was the day of the turntablist competition. He didn't want me to go with him. The second was Mama telling me she was going for a workshop in Ho and wouldn't be back until evening.

I didn't know what to do with myself. I wondered if anyone would notice if I went to campus and continued weeding. The rule book said day students were not allowed on campus during non-teaching hours. I decided it was too risky. I tidied my room and did the laundry. Mama had locked her bedroom door, so I couldn't even steal back my laptop.

On impulse, I decided to go to Vume. Maybe if I was lucky, I could get to see someone making the pots. I changed into jeans and a T-shirt, stuffed some money into my pocket and walked to the roadside. Getting a *trotro* turned out to be difficult. It was only *okada* riders who honked and asked if I wanted a ride. When I did get a *trotro* it took us twenty minutes to get to Vume.

I walked to the stall from which I had bought my first vase, but there were none like it there. Now that I knew how tricky working with clay was, I was amazed at how symmetrical and perfect the pots were. I couldn't believe they'd all been made by hand. I walked down the road, stopping to look at designs, shapes and colours. Each time I got to a new stall, an attendant got up, but I signalled that I was only looking and they returned to their seats.

I was so engrossed in examining an earthenware pot in one of the smaller stalls that I didn't see the attendant until he asked, "May I help you?"

"No, I'm just looking," I said putting the pot back. All the pots had the same red earth colour. None had the fanciful colouring of the pots that were closer to the roadside.

"Hey, I know you," I said recognizing the boy. "You're the one who helped us with our things."

The boy smiled sheepishly. "I'm the one who broke your vase. My name is Ahmad."

"I'm Yayra. Did you make these?"

He shook his head. "No. My brother did. He and my grandmother. I handle the sales. I'm studying business in Comboni High."

"Jamal's your brother?"

"Yes, you know him?"

Now that he had said Jamal was his brother, I could see the resemblance. It wasn't really in the physical looks but in their mannerisms: the way they used they hands to gesture when they talked, the way they cocked their head to one side, their intonations and inflections.

"We go to school together."

"Oh."

His 'oh' said a lot. It said he knew I had heard the rumours and it dared me to say something.

"Is he home?"

"Jamal?"

Duh? Who were we talking about? I nodded. "I want to say 'hi'."

Ahmad looked surprised but he pointed to a house a little distance from the road. "He's just returned from bringing clay from the pits."

I walked past him into the town proper. Oyster shells embedded in the ground formed some sort of pavement. There were pots everywhere. Large pots for storing water stood lined up along the outer walls of buildings. Some of the buildings were made from clay. A few had thatch roofs, others had aluminium roofing sheets. Some of the houses had beautiful flower pots in front of them. Almost every compound had an outdoor kitchen; most of the utensils I saw were made from clay. Goats, dogs, sheep and chickens roamed freely in the village. They didn't even get out of the way when I approached.

Jamal's home was one of those built with cement blocks

and had an aluminium sheet roof. I could hear hip-life music coming from one of the rooms. There wasn't an outdoor kitchen.

I called out, "*Agoo, agoo.*"

A cute little girl, about two-years-old, came running from behind the house. She was giggling and seemed to be running away from someone. She stopped and stared when she saw me. There were streaks of toothpaste on her face and arms. Her cheeks dimpled when she smiled. Seconds after she appeared, Jamal appeared behind her, a small toothbrush was in his hand. Like the little girl, he just stood there and stared at me.

"Hi," I said awkwardly.

It was one thing seeing him in school in his uniform. It was quite another seeing him bare-chested with his boxers peeking out of his shorts. Sofi was right, he was very cute.

"Uh, hi."

"Daddy, up, up," the little girl said.

"Say 'please'."

"Please Daddy, up, up," the girl said.

Jamal reached down and swung her over his head. She shrieked in delight.

"I saw your brother, Ahmad. He told me you were home, so I decided to say 'hi' and to thank you for the *langa-langa*. I think I'll finish weeding by Thursday."

"Is that why you came here? To Vume?" he asked and his voice had an edge to it.

"I came because Miss Naa said we should we come. I thought

I might find someone making pots and watch them."

"Is that the only reason?"

"What other reason could there be?"

"I don't know? You tell me. Maybe you came to see if what everyone was saying about me was true."

"I didn't even know you lived here," I said getting angry, "and in case you hadn't realized you aren't the only one people are talking about!" I turned and walked out of the compound. What had I been thinking? Just because he had been nice enough to bring me the *langa-langa* didn't mean he wanted us to be friends. Maybe he had brought it to make up for the vase his brother broke.

I walked past Ahmad and didn't stop when he called me. I crossed over to the other side of the street. Each *trotro* that passed was full. Some *okada* riders asked if I wanted a ride. I shook my head.

I turned away when I saw Jamal coming towards me. He had put on a T-shirt. The little girl was following him. When they got to the roadside, Ahmad picked her up. She started crying and shouting 'Daddy, Daddy'. I prayed a *trotro* would stop before Jamal crossed over but none did.

He walked and stood right in front of me. I ignored him and concentrated on flagging a *trotro*.

"I'm sorry."

I ignored him and continued flagging down the buses. They all passed by me.

"Don't go please. At least, stay for what you came for. I'll show you how we make the pots. If you're angry with me, I'll have my grandmother show you."

A trotro was approaching us with blinking indicator lights. It came to a stop not far from where I stood. The driver's mate got down. A woman and two children also got down and went to the boot where the mate took out their bags.

"I'm so used to people treating me like an outcast that I don't even know what to do when someone is being nice to me. I really am sorry. Please don't go."

The mate turned to me and asked if I was leaving.

Jamal held his breath.

I shook my head. The mate hit the side of the bus and shouted, 'Away' before jumping into the moving bus.

Jamal exhaled. A crooked smile appeared on his face. I followed him across the street where he picked his whimpering daughter from Ahmad, and we went back into his compound.

"I lied to you," he said when we went inside.

"It's a market day. My grandmother's gone to the market. So you're stuck with me."

I rolled my eyes. He laughed. His daughter laughed too and he tickled her tummy which made her laugh even more.

"I was trying to get her to brush her teeth, but she just wanted to play with the clay. Maybe now that you're here she'll behave. She's such a show-off."

He spoke with so much pride in his voice that I couldn't believe he'd have given his girlfriend a concoction to kill their unborn baby. The little girl indeed was a show-off. She stood obediently while Jamal brushed her teeth. She swallowed some of the toothpaste initially, but then she spat the lather out and rinsed when Jamal asked her to.

"Who's a good girl?" he asked her when they were done brushing.

"Soraia" she squealed and clapped her hands.

Jamal led me to a shed behind the house. There were no oyster shells there. He showed me the basket of clay he had dug up that morning. There were bits and pieces of rocks, leaves and sticks in it. Miss Naa's hand-outs explained all about the processing of clay so I knew he'd later pound the clay until it became as smooth as powder. Then he would sieve it to get rid of the impurities, soak it for a couple of days and then drain off the water. What remained would be stored until it was ready to be used.

"If you already know how to make pots, why are you in Miss Naa's class?"

"To learn how to use the wheel. Pots made on the wheel are the only type that can be glazed."

He took a ball of clay from a plastic bucket and began kneading it on a board. He looked at me and realized I didn't understand what he had said. "Traditional pots are heavier. Their firing style is different than for pots produced on the wheel. Glazed pots require higher temperatures. Temperatures you can only get in a kiln."

He cut sections of the clay and began rolling them into ropes. Soraia was playing with a ball of clay. He kept an eye on her as he rolled.

"But those pots by the road side; they come in different colours."

"They're sprayed with car paint."

"Oh," I said. "What does a glazed pot look like?"

"The vase Ahmad broke? That was glazed."

I remembered how shiny and smooth the vase had been. How it had reminded me of glass.

Jamal laid the first rope of clay on the bare ground in a circular pattern. He ran his finger around the bottom of the inside and outside of the rope to help it to stick to the ground. He took another rope of clay and carefully placed it on the first rope while walking backwards. He alternately pulled up the clay and smoothed it with one hand while guiding and supporting the clay rope with the other. In no time at all by successively adding ropes of clay he had made the top half of a pot. With quick, deft strokes he used a piece of broken calabash to smooth the walls and shape the pot. He spent a bit more time on the mouth. His eyebrows were furrowed in concentration, just like they had been when he was working on the potter's wheel in the ceramics studio. Even Soraia stopped playing and watched her father work.

"We leave it to dry a little then we turn it onto its mouth and make the bottom."

"I didn't know they made them in two parts."

He shrugged, like it wasn't a big deal.

"Do you want to try?"

I shook my head. "I wouldn't get it right."

"I'm only good because I've been doing this since I was three."

I shook my head.

"I'm not going to grade you. Here take it."

I hesitated but I took the rope of clay he offered. I couldn't even put the clay down in a perfect circle. He gave me another rope of clay and I placed it on the first one in much the same way as he had, pulling and smoothing as I went along. By the time I had got to the neck of the pot, one wall was in danger of collapsing.

"It's never going to be perfect."

"It doesn't have to be," Jamal said, looking at me.

"But yours is so perfect."

"It only appears perfect to you, but to a trained eye there are so many imperfections. Even if you do get the perfect pot, you can't control what will happen during the firing process. Pots may crack or break or anything . . . They're never perfect. Just like human beings. Just like life."

He took the broken piece of calabash and gently reshaped my pot. He used one hand to wipe sweat off his brow and left a streak of clay on his forehead.

"You have clay on your face," I said.

He looked up from my pot and looked at his hand. It was all clayey. He slid it down the left side of my face.

"Now you have clay on your face too," he said and grinned.

Soraia must have thought it was a new game and smeared

clay on her face as well.

"I guess we're all clay people," I said.

"I don't remember exactly, but there's a tribe who say they came out of the ground."

"A hole in the ground," I corrected pompously, "and it's the Asantes."

"The ground, a hole in the ground, what's the difference?" Jamal asked, unimpressed.

Soraia showed me the lump of clay she had in her hand. She had made an opening of some sort in it.

"Cup," she said with authority daring me to disagree that the object she held in her hand was anything but a cup.

"Cup," I repeated.

She seemed satisfied with that and went back to moulding her clay.

"You're wonderful with her," I said, surprising myself, but I couldn't stop talking. "My Dad was like that with me. It's my fault he died. We were coming home from school, and I said I wanted fast food. My mother doesn't allow us to eat fast food so we always did it behind her back. Daddy didn't want to go, but I insisted and then we had the accident. She doesn't say it but I know she blames me."

He looked from me to Soraia. "Sometimes I think if we hadn't had her, if Lebene didn't get pregnant, she wouldn't have had to drop out of school and she would still be alive. I blamed myself for her death for a long time but then I realized she had made a choice. Getting Lebene pregnant was a mistake but going ahead to have Soraia wasn't. We didn't ever want her to think she was a mistake. It's why we named her Soraia. It means princess."

We both looked over to where the princess was bathing herself with slurry.

"Your mom doesn't blame you. Sometimes we make bad choices and have to live with the consequences."

I wondered what had made me bare my soul to him. Whatever it was that had compelled me, I felt much better than I had ever since the fight in school.

Chapter

12

I washed my face and went to wait with Ahmad, while Jamal and Soraia took a bath.

"Jamal fixed that Cardew guy's old potter's wheel. Did he tell you?"

"Michael Cardew?"

"Yeah, he worked here in this town. His wheel requires an assistant, someone to be cranking a handle to spin the wheel, but it was so old that once, when Jamal was working and I was turning it, it just broke. He hasn't been able to fix it again. I guess it's too old. He was experimenting with glazes. That vase I broke was one of his."

"The guy I bought it from said the clay was from far away."

"That's the line Abdul uses. No one in town knows they're Jamal's work. If they knew, those pots wouldn't get sold. I mean after everything that happened with Lebene, people just . . ., you know. . ."

I nodded. I did know.

"He said glazed pots needed high temperatures, where did he fire them?"

Ahmad looked at me for a moment. "Promise you won't tell?"

I nodded.

"In your school. He used to sneak there on weekends to use the kiln. One day this student from KNUST found him in the studio. She said she was going to teach in your school for a year. She didn't report him though; he would have got into a lot of trouble. She took five of his pieces and sold them for him at an art exhibition in Kumasi. The prices she sold them at were unbelievable!"

"Miss Naa?"

"You know her? It was she who convinced him to switch courses. He wasn't really into science. She wants him to apply to KNUST when he graduates. She says he has lots of potential."

"Wow," I said.

"I'm glad you're his friend. I know he pretends he doesn't care what people think about him but he does. He made one mistake and people judge him like they don't do worse things themselves. It's not easy for him. My grandmother works but she's old, and these pots don't sell as fast as the sprayed type. He's putting us through school, taking care of Soraia, the bills, what we eat . . . He doesn't say it, but I know it's not easy for him. We do all the odd jobs we can get during vacation so we can pay our fees and stuff. You know we're not even real brothers?"

"Huh?"

"I mean we're step-brothers. Different mothers, same father. My dad had three wives. My mom was the most senior; she died when I was small, and Jamal's mother took me in. Then my dad divorced her, and she brought me with her when she was coming here. She taught him to make pots."

Ahmad stopped talking when Jamal and Soraia came out on a motorcycle. Jamal was dressed for work. Soraia looked extra pretty in a blue and yellow flowery dress. This time she went straight to Ahmad without complaining.

"I have the afternoon shift at work. Climb on; I'll drop you off at your home."

"I'm not riding that thing," I said.

"I won't go fast."

"No."

He parked the motorcycle, went back into the house and returned with two helmets.

"I'll take a *trotro*."

"It's a market day; most of them will be full. Come on."

Despite my better judgement, I did climb onto the motorbike. Jamal put a helmet onto my head and secured it. He wore one too. After waving to Soraia and Ahmad, we set off with me holding on to him for dear life. He pointed out the Cardew kiln to me.

He kept his word and rode really slowly. Once we got across the Sogakofe Bridge he increased his speed until I thought we were flying in the wind. I screamed at him to slow down, but he just laughed and ignored me. I kept expecting us to crash into something and scenes from the accident with Daddy kept flashing before my eyes. Most of it was still a blur but I distinctly remembered the fear—my fear of dying, the fear I felt when I saw Daddy bleeding and my fear as he died before my eyes. When Jamal parked in front of our bungalow I got down, removed the helmet and hit him with it. Hard.

"What's wrong with you?! Are you insane?!" I asked. There were tears in my eyes and though I kept blinking, I couldn't stop them from running down my face.

"Do you think it's funny? Do you think being in an accident is funny? I lost my father! He died because some idiot like you was doing 90kph on a 50kph road. My Dad swerved to avoid hitting him and we ended up somersaulting and hitting a cement wall. The car engine landed right in our laps. They had to cut us out of the car with machines. I watched my Dad die, and there was nothing I could do. Nothing anyone could do. I watched him die. He bled to death. There was blood everywhere, and I couldn't even touch him. He was calling my name, and I couldn't even hold him!"

Jamal got off his bike and tried to hold me.

"Don't touch me!" I yelled.

"I'm sorry. I didn't realize . . ."

"I kept asking you to stop, to slow down, but you didn't mind me!"

"Yayra, I really am sorry. I didn't . . ."

I walked past him to the front door, unlocked it and entered leaving him standing out there in the yard. He rang the doorbell five times. I ignored him. He gave up and rode away.

*

Mama came home at about five. I pretended to be asleep when she came in to check on me. At about six I heard a motorbike in our yard. Minutes later the doorbell rang. I heard Jamal greet Mama and ask if he could see me. I heard Mama tell him I was asleep.

*

I stayed in bed the whole of Sunday. I told Mama I had cramps. She went to church alone. Jamal came by in the morning. I heard the bike, I heard the doorbell ring. I let it ring. He came by again in the evening. Mama told him I was still not well.

*

Monday at break Jamal came to the plot. I ignored him. He kept apologizing, and I knew he was sorry, but that ride had almost been like reliving the accident. I poured out all my anger on the grass and weeded a sizable portion.

*

When I got home from school that day Mama was waiting for me.

"Are you okay?"

What did she care whether I was okay or not? She still hadn't asked me what had led to the fight with Sefakor.

"That young man who keeps coming here did he . . . did he do anything to you?"

I stared at her.

"Did he try to force you to do anything you didn't want to do?"

"Did he rape me you mean?"

"Yes, did he?"

"No."

"The security men said he brought you home on Saturday. They said he has something of a reputation, and I don't want you to get hurt."

Did my mother not have any idea how her own behaviour was hurting me? Did she not know what I was going through in school? How could she be completely clueless?

"I don't want you seeing him anymore. From now onwards, the driver will take you right up to the school gate. When you close, he'll pick you up from the school and bring you straight home."

"Mama . . ."

"This isn't up for discussion. Is that clear?" Boys like that are trouble. They don't know what they want."

I knew then that this was my real punishment for getting into a fight in school.

*

Jamal marched straight up to me before assembly the next day. He was seething. "What did you tell your mother about me? The security men wouldn't let me enter the hospital."

"I didn't tell her anything."

"They said I hurt you."

"I didn't tell her anything."

"Don't you think I'm suffering enough with what happened to Lebene? And now I have to deal with this too!"

"I didn't . . ."

He walked away from me.

I finished weeding my plot that day and called the assistant headmaster to inspect it. The internal suspension was lifted. I went to class the next day, but nothing changed. No one spoke to me or looked in my direction. Not even Allison.

Chapter

13

I kept going to the ceramics studio at break. It was always empty. I was rolling out ropes for a pot one day when the door swung open. Jamal marched straight up to me. He stood right in my face and said through clenched teeth, "Go on, ask me."

"Ask you what?"

"Ask me if it's true."

"Ask you if what is true?"

"Ask me about Lebene's death. About her baby."

"It's not my business."

He raised his left hand and it came slamming down onto the wall behind me. "Ask me," he seethed.

"Miss Naa said there's no past nor future in this room. There's only the present—the now. Nothing else matters."

He dragged me out of the room. There was no point in resisting. I suspect he would have carried me out if he had had to.

"Ask me," he said once we were outside and he had propped me against the wall.

"It wouldn't change anything."

"Why? Because you've already judged me and decided you know the truth?"

"No. Because the police said you didn't do it."

He laughed. There was no gaiety in the laughter. It was dry and bitter.

"The police *said* there was insufficient evidence to arrest me," he corrected. He was looking at me with barely concealed rage. His nostrils flared with each breath he took. His breathing was heavy and rugged. "Ask me."

"I said it doesn't matter."

"You haven't heard my version. I'm not leaving till you ask me." His eyes bore deep into me.

I relented. I wanted to finish my pot before break was over. "Did you give her the herbal concoction to drink?"

He looked at me, long and hard. "No."

"Did you leave the spa that night?"

"Yes, for about fifteen minutes." His eyes never left mine.

"Did you meet up with Lebene?"

"Yes."

I gasped. "Where?"

"By the river."

I sputtered and nearly choked when I asked, "Why?"

"She asked me to."

"Why?"

"To tell me she was pregnant. To tell me she didn't want to keep it."

"Was it your baby?"

He looked at me again with a look of what? Regret? Hurt? Disappointment?

"*You* asked me to ask you," I reminded him.

He sighed and dropped his hand as if regretting his prior insistence that I question him. "No. I hadn't slept with her since Soraia. After my parents divorced, my mom moved us to Vume from Takoradi. I was upset about their divorce; I was more upset about moving to a village. I thought it was her fault that my dad had left her. She was always nagging him about where he'd been, who he had been with, that kind of thing. I started running with a group of wild guys; drinking, smoking, staying out late. I knew Lebene from school but we were not close or anything. Then we met at a party, I was drunk . . . I know that's not an excuse but . . ."

He stopped talking and watched my face intently. Then he looked away.

"Two months later she told me she was pregnant. By the time Soraia was born, my mother was sick. She couldn't work anymore. Then she died. I dropped out of school to work. That's the story. That's my story."

He turned and leaned against the wall so that we were standing side by side. He looked tired.

"That night—at the spa, what did she want?"

"She just wanted to talk. She didn't know what to do. She

said her parents would kill her if they found out."

"Did she tell you who the father was?"

"No. She only said he was a married businessman. He had children."

"Why didn't you tell the police?"

He laughed another dry and bitter laugh.

"Yeah, right! Like they'd have believed me—a school drop-out, an ex-*wee* smoker, a teenage father. Do you think they were seriously going to look for this mysterious businessman because *I* said so?"

He sighed. We stood in silence for a long time.

"Why did you want me to ask you?"

He turned and looked at me. He ran his finger along the scar on the dead part of my face. I didn't feel anything of course, but that didn't stop my heart from galloping.

He was silent for a long time. "I'm tired of pretending I don't care what people think. Maybe I really don't care what people think but I care what *you* think. That day you came to visit? I guess I had forgotten what it felt like to have a friend."

He walked away, while I stood by the wall trying to get my breath back. "Jamal wait!" I called, running after him.

"What?"

"We can still be friends."

"Your mom said I wasn't to speak to you."

"You met my mom?"

"She was at the spa last week. She was kind of under the impression that I tried to rape you or something."

"My mother she's just so . . . she tries to control everything and when it doesn't go according to her plan, she freaks out. Instead of asking why I was upset with you, she just assumed you had tried to force me into something."

He shrugged.

"She's not here. She won't know if we're friends or not."

"What if I want to be more than friends?"

I looked away. Was he asking me out?

"Yayra, I'm nineteen. I'm not a child anymore. If this thing with you gets out and some other girl makes up a story about rape, it will be my word against hers and who's going to believe me? Where will that leave Soraia or Ahmad or my grandmother? I can't afford to make any more mistakes. Look, I shouldn't have come. I'm sorry."

"Sorry for what? For needing a friend? For not being made of stone? Everyone needs a friend, Jamal."

Just then Komi Mensah passed in front of the ceramics department to the sculpture department. We both looked at him as he passed. Jamal lifted a hand in greeting. Komi ignored him.

"Not everyone," Jamal said and walked away. This time I didn't go after him.

*

I continued going to the ceramics room at break time. Jamal never came by, not even during extracurricular class. Sometimes I saw Komi on his way to the sculpture department. Once after school, when the driver was late, I saw him working on one of the sculptures in the arboretum. Whatever it was he had begun working on still hadn't taken shape but I noticed the sculpture of the three monkey heads depicting, 'see no evil, hear no evil, speak no evil' bore his name. I wondered if any other student had noticed how gifted he was. Anytime I saw him after that I called him by name and waved. He never waved back.

*

I was working on my pot during break one morning when Jamal came in. He looked worried.

"Hi," he said.

"Hi," I said back.

"May I borrow your phone please? I need to make a call. Soraia got a fever and my grandmother sent her to the hospital this morning. I want to know if she's okay. Our lights were off the whole of yesterday, I couldn't charge my phone."

I took it out of my pocket and gave it to him. He stepped out of the room and came back in moments later more worried than when he stepped out.

"They've admitted her. My grandma says she'll call back. They're trying to set a drip on her." He looked so worried that I knew he had meant it when he had said that even if Soraia's conception had been a mistake, taking the decision to have her could never have been a mistake.

"She'll be fine. My mom's a paediatrician. She's one of the best there is. She'll take really good care of her."

"I . . . I can't help worrying. I came this morning to ask

permission to be absented but Mr Amedoda refused. I couldn't cut class because he kept coming into my class every two minutes to check to see if I was in. I feel so useless."

"My mom's really good. When she was the head of the paediatric department in Korle bu, her department always got the 'Best Department' award. She got the 'Best Paediatrician' award three times running till she told them to stop giving it to her so someone else could be recognized. She loves children; she hates to see them in pain. Soraia will be fine."

He sat and watched me mould my pot.

"The thing on your stomach, does it hurt?"

"The stoma? No. Most times I don't even realize it's there. Does it disgust you?"

"When my mom was sick they had to put a tube through her nose so they could feed her. She even had to wear diapers. Sometimes, when the nurses were overworked, I cleaned and bathed her. Besides, I've changed Soraia's diapers like a zillion times."

"What happened to your mom?"

"Breast cancer."

"Sorry."

He nodded. "What happened to you?"

"Inflammatory bowel disease. It means I had sores in my colon. I got very bad abdominal cramps, very bad pain and severe diarrhoea. I used to go to the toilet like ten, fifteen times a day. More times in the night. The stool was always bloody. It got so bad that I got anaemia and needed blood transfusions on a number of occasions. After my last transfusion my mother put her foot down and I had surgery to remove my colon. I might have surgery to have it reversed later on if I want. My mom says the reversal is my choice."

"What causes it?"

I shrugged. "It's an autoimmune thing. My body attacks itself."

"Must be hard."

"Not anymore. But the great thing is I don't have to rush for the toilet even if I get diarrhoea. Remember my friend from the spa? The short one?"

He smiled. "The one who dresses like a rainbow? It's kind of hard not to notice her."

I laughed, "Yeah, that's Sofi for you. That last night . . ."

"The night of your birthday?"

"No, it wasn't my birthday. My birthday was the Monday of that week."

"The day I found you—?"

"I have a fully functioning memory, thank you. I know what I was doing when you found me."

He raised his hands, "Easy, don't bite."

"I thought you were going to tease me about crying. I was watching videos of my Dad. It's why I bring the phone to school. I like to hear his voice when I'm having a really bad day. Anyway, that night at the spa, Sofi ate a bit of my food, Dede's food and her onion soup. Then she had cake, ice cream and a fruit salad with milk. She was running like a tap the next day. Mama had to give her some Imodium before they went back to Accra."

"Why did you move here?"

I bit my lip. "We didn't have any money for my school fees or the rent. My dad, he was like a 'Good Samaritan'. My mom says he lent money out to people who never paid back and he made some bad investments. We were broke when he died. Mama heard about the job here and there were great benefits, so we came."

"You couldn't have been all that broke. The three of you spent like two thousand cedis at the spa that weekend."

"Huh?"

"Your bill was almost two thousand cedis. I checked."

"Why?"

He shrugged. "I wanted to see what rich, spoilt girls did for fun."

"You think I'm a 'rich, spoilt girl'?"

"How many people in this school do you think use iPhones or iPods or MacBook Pros?"

I shrugged. I wouldn't apologize for that. "Dad was crazy about Apple products. He had to get every new product that came off their assembly line. When he got tired of them he gave them to me, but most times they got lost or stolen. He was always forgetting them when he went out. His carelessness used to drive Mama crazy."

"I guess I judged you without knowing you."

"And now what do you think."

"That you're just like everyone else; just trying to make some sense out of your life."

"Trying to make the imperfect perfect," I said, straightening the wall of my lopsided pot.

"But what if the imperfect is perfect the way it is? What if the imperfect didn't have to be made perfect?"

"Huh?"

"What if that pot is perfect the way it is with its warped wall? If you fired it the way it is, it would still be able to hold water. Isn't that what matters? That it fulfils its function? Why must both walls be symmetrical? Besides your view of perfection may be another person's imperfection. So perfection, like beauty depends, on the beholder. Logically, that would mean *nothing* is perfect and, therefore, *everything* is imperfect."

"Wow, where did all this philosophy for come from all of a sudden?"

"Just think about it for a minute. Who defines what perfect is? I mean why can't perfect be—having scars on your face, or being overweight, or having prominent teeth?"

My phone rang. He had hit a little too close to home with his last comment.

"It's my grandmother," he said walking out.

I was staring at my imperfect pot when he walked back into the class. Mr Amedoda was with him. My phone was in Mr Amedoda's hand.

"I knew you were up to no good. Whose phone is this?"

"I already told you, it's mine," Jamal said. His face had

settled into an unreadable mask.

"You want me to believe you own a pink phone which has an orange case with yellow butterflies and smileys? What? You think I'm stupid?"

"It's mine," Jamal insisted.

"Young man, don't add petrol to fire," Mr Amedoda warned.

"It's mine," I said getting up from the desk.

"The headmistress' office! Now!" Mr Amedoda barked.

Chapter
14

Mama didn't say a word when she came to pick me up. My two week external suspension began with immediate effect. I was going to get it big time, I could see it from the way her lips had settled into a straight line. Her grip on the steering wheel was so firm that I could see the veins sticking out on the back of her hands.

"You are not to step out of this compound for the next two weeks. Is that clear?" she asked, as she dropped me off at home.

I nodded and got out of the car.

I put my laptop and iPod in Mama's room. She already had my phone. I went to my room and tried to sleep but I couldn't. I was worried about Soraia. Jamal hadn't even got round to hearing what his grandmother had called to say before he got busted. He had gone for his bag and left the campus, while I had waited for Mama to come and get me.

I took out Daddy's jumper and buried my face in it. His smell was almost all gone. I took off my uniform and pulled on the jumper. Then I lay in bed waiting for Mama to close from work.

I heard her slam the door shut when she entered three hours later. That was never a good sign. I heard her throw her hand-bag down onto the table. Her keys followed. I was in big time trouble.

"Yayra!" she called in her 'don't mess with me' voice. There was no use pretending to be asleep. She'd probably walk into my room and pull me out of bed. She was pacing in the living room. Pacing was the mother of all bad signs.

"Yes?" I said.

She turned to look at me; her mouth was open but the words never made it past her throat. Seeing me in Daddy's jumper must have done something to her.

"Go and change and come back here," she ordered in a voice so tight I thought it would snap.

"I won't change," I said.

"Don't start that. Go and change and come back here."

"Start what? Talking about Daddy? Why do you hate talking about him so much? Why do you want us to pretend that he never lived? If you have something to say to me, just say it. I'm not changing."

"You want to talk about your father? Fine! He had another woman in Sakumono. He had FOUR CHILDREN with her! He built them a house, a SIX-BEDROOM HOUSE while we lived in a rented place! You think he was perfect? He wasn't. He was a two-timing bastard! Everything was a lie. Everything he ever told us. Everything he ever did. All those times he said he was travelling here for Easter and funerals, he never came. He hadn't set foot in Sogakofe in FIFTEEN YEARS! He spent that time with his other family! The family he emptied our bank account, our savings—my savings, to build a house for, and take care of."

I felt the breath whoosh out of my body like someone had punched me in the gut. "You're lying, Daddy would NEVER do that!"

She seemed to run out of steam after her revelation. She deflated right before my very eyes. She suddenly looked overworked and tired. She looked nothing like the woman who had had everything going according to her big plan.

"Ask anyone. Ask Uncle Larweh or Aunt Cee. Ask your cousin Samuel. Call them and ask," she said softly, covering her mouth with a trembling hand, as if she couldn't believe the words she had uttered earlier had come out of her own mouth.

"You're lying," I said. I only realized how hard I was also shaking when my teeth started chattering. I hated myself for crying but I couldn't stop the tears. It felt like a dam somewhere inside of me had broken and the water was gushing out. The pain I felt in my heart was worse than any physical pain I'd ever felt. It was a million times worse than the pain I'd felt when I was trapped in our wrecked car with Daddy lying dead, a hand's breadth away from me.

"I'm sorry. I didn't want you to find out this way. I'm so sorry," Mama said. She came to me and tried to hug me.

"Don't touch me!" I screamed and backed away from her. "Don't you dare touch me! I hate you! I wish it was you who'd died that day!"

I ran to my room, slammed the door hard and locked it behind me.

How dare she say something like that about him? My father would never do anything like that to us. He'd never do that to me. How could she even say those things about him?

Mama followed me to my room. I heard her turn the door handle. She stood there for maybe five minutes. I don't know what she was doing. Truth was I didn't care. I heard her go to her room. She came back to my door and left something in front of it and then she returned to her room. I cried myself to sleep.

*

I woke up at dawn the next morning. Though I tried to, I couldn't go back to sleep. It couldn't be true. Daddy couldn't do that to us. He wouldn't. But then I remembered things that had happened when he was alive. Once when I was eight I had found a black doll in his wardrobe. I'd thought he was hiding it from me until my birthday. On my birthday it hadn't been among my gifts. I had asked him about it, but he had laughed and said I had been so excited about my birthday that I had dreamt it.

I also remembered that he had had a password on his phone. When I asked why, he said it was so that even if it got lost or stolen, whoever found it would not be able to use it. Daddy had seldom got angry but he used to get very pissed off whenever his phone rang and I answered. It got to the point that if he was not around and his phone rang, neither Mama nor I would answer.

All those times he had claimed he had misplaced his phone or laptop, had he just given them to his other kids? I thought back to our first visit to DJ's house and remembered how DJ had said he had never seen my father at Easter.

The tears came hot and fast. How could he have done that to us? To me? To Mama? Mama? I realized the house was unusually quiet. I always woke up to the sound of Mama doing her aerobics in front of the TV. Today there was nothing. I heard movement in her room, so I knew she was awake. Why wasn't she exercising? How long had she known about this other woman and her four children? I hadn't been fair to her at all. I had blamed her for everything when all she was guilty of was shielding me from the truth. She had even paid for a birthday gift that we hadn't been able to afford. I had told her I hated her. What was worse, I had said I wished she was the one that died that day.

At 6 a.m. she came out of her room.

Please knock on my door. Call my name. Show me you're not angry.

Mama didn't call me. She didn't even stop in front of my door like she had the night before. I heard the front door open and close behind her. I heard her car start. She drove away. I lay on my bed for hours until my stomach rumbled. I was starving. I hadn't had lunch or supper the previous day. I opened the door and almost fell. I had stumbled over my laptop, my phone and iPod.

It was only after I'd eaten some leftover rice and beans stew that I remembered Jamal and Soraia. I tried the number Jamal had dialled on my phone, but the recorded voice said the phone was switched off. I changed out of Daddy's jumper into jeans and a T-shirt and hurried to the paediatric ward. Having your mother as the medical superintendent had its advantages. I wouldn't have to wait until visiting hours to see Soraia.

The walls of the ward had pictures of alphabets, numbers, animals, cartoon and nursery rhyme characters. It almost looked like a kindergarten. The nurse I met at the reception was one I knew from my morning rides on the hospital bus.

"Hi, can I see Soraia please. Soraia Abdullah."

The nurse pointed to a side ward and I made my way there.

"There, that's a good girl," a voice I knew very well said.

"Soraia is good girl," I heard Soraia say.

"Yes, Soraia is a very good girl."

I peeped through the open door. Mama's back was towards me. She was bent over Soraia's crib; her stethoscope was in her ears. She checked Soraia's chest and wrote something on a chart. An IV infusion line had been attached to the back of Soraia's left hand.

"Auntie," Soraia called out when she saw me.

Mama turned.

"You said I couldn't step out of the hospital compound. You

didn't say I couldn't step out of the house."

"I know what I said."

"I only wanted to make sure she was okay."

Mama nodded.

"Will she be okay?"

"Yeah, she'll stay here for a bit but she'll be fine."

"Auntie, Soraia have hurt here," she said, pointing to the needle in her small hand.

Mama smiled, "She's shown that to everyone who's entered this ward—the nurses, the orderlies, even other kids' visitors."

I smiled back at her. "Jamal calls her a 'show-off'."

"Have you seen him?"

"Jamal? No."

"He's asleep in my office. He was up with her the whole night. Go and see if he's awake, I'm sure Soraia would love to see him."

I turned to go but stopped at the door.

"Mama I . . . I didn't mean what I said last night."

"I know," she said, but she wasn't looking at me. She was arranging the papers in Soraia's folder.

I went and stood right in front of her. It was only then that I saw the tears in her eyes.

"Mama, I really am sorry. I don't hate you. I don't wish you had died."

She nodded and wiped her face. "I know. I have rounds to make, let's talk about this later, okay?"

*

Jamal was dead to the world when I entered Mama's office. He was asleep on her sofa. He was still in his school uniform. He had come straight to be by Soraia's side after his suspension. I sat on one of the chairs by the sofa and watched him sleep.

Were there any perfect people? How long would Daddy have lied to us? What of his other kids? What had he told them each time he was coming home to us?

I sighed. Jamal must have been sleeping with his ears open because he woke up and jumped off the sofa. "Soraia?"

"She's fine. My mom's with her."

He rubbed his eyes and lay back.

"You can go back to sleep, Mama says you didn't get any sleep last night."

"*I* didn't get any sleep? *She* was the one sponging Soraia all through the night. She only left at dawn and that was to take a bath and change. We had a long chat about everything: my mom, Lebene, the suspension. She's really nice."

"We had a fight last night and I said some really nasty things to her. Turns out my 'perfect' dad had another woman. Turns out I have four step-siblings. Turns out he built them a house with his and Mama's savings; that's the real reason we're broke. That story about him being a 'Good Samaritan' was a lie Mama made up."

"Are you okay?"

"I'll live. It's Mama that I feel sorry for. I can't even begin to imagine what she's feeling. I mean when I was discharged from the hospital, I hated her for carrying on as if everything was all right. I didn't know it was all an act. I didn't know she was being strong for me. She never said one bad word about him. Never. She was protecting me from who he was and I was busy hating her and feeling sorry for myself."

"At least you know the truth now."

I nodded and headed towards the door.

"Hey guess who was brought to the ER yesterday?"

"Who?"

"Sefakor Deku. Komi Mensah bit her on the face twice. The story is all over town. They say she called him 'vampire' and he just lost it. He grabbed her and bit her or should I say he sunk his fangs into her? I overheard some nurses say she needed stitches and that she might have terrible scars."

I laughed so hard my sides hurt. Jamal looked confused.

"Don't you see? She's also a vampire now. When humans get bitten by vampires they get transformed into vampires!"

Jamal chuckled and followed me to Soraia's ward.

Chapter
15

"Mama?" I opened her door. She lay prone oh her bed. She had spent the entire day and most of the night in the hospital. She had come home ten minutes earlier and had a bath. A stream of light from the corridor lit up her dark room.

"Yes?"

In the darkness I saw her lift herself up on her elbows. I approached her bed and sat at the edge.

"When did you find out? About Dad."

She rubbed her eyes and sat up straighter. I was glad for the cover of darkness. I didn't think I could bear to see the hurt in her eyes. I still hadn't got over seeing her cry. All my life I'd seen my mother as a strong woman. Seeing that she was vulnerable was very unsettling.

"After the funeral. The woman came to me and said she wanted his property to be shared equally among all five of his children. She had their birth certificates, pictures of them together and letters he had written. She didn't believe me when I said there was nothing to inherit, so she sent the case to court. I got subpoenaed to present our bank records. They found out there was nothing. He hadn't left anything."

I folded the ends of her sleeping cloth into pleats wondering how I had been so wrapped up in myself that I hadn't noticed what was happening. "I didn't even know you went to court."

"You were going through so much and I didn't want you to have to worry about that."

"Did you know? Did you suspect there was someone else?"

She shook her head. "No."

She lifted up a part of her sleeping cloth—a clear invitation for me to climb in beside her. I was only too happy to oblige. I snuggled into her side like I had many times as a child when I had had a bad dream and was too scared to sleep on my own. Though I was no more a six-year-old, I still felt safe cocooned in her embrace.

"What happened to us? We used to be so close. If Jamal hadn't spoken to me, I wouldn't have known why you got suspended; I wouldn't have known you blamed yourself for Daddy's death. It's not your fault he died. It was an accident. No more secrets from tonight, okay?"

I nodded, relieved. "Do you hate him?"

She was silent for so long that I thought she had fallen asleep.

"Sometimes I think that if he miraculously came back to life, I'd strangle him with my bare hands. Other times I think that if he had been honest with me, maybe I'd have forgiven him. But most times—most times, I wonder why we were not enough. Why *I* wasn't enough."

"I'm so sorry. I thought he was *so* perfect."

She drew the cloth over my bare arm.

"Only God is perfect. Everyone has flaws, but that doesn't mean we shouldn't strive for perfection. The important thing is not to pretend to be something we're not and to realize that we're beautiful even with our flaws."

"We're all perfectly imperfect," I said as I drifted off to sleep.

Later that year . . .

I sat staring at the quiz mistress, Professor Elsie Kauffman, at the finals of the National Maths and Science Quiz. Sogakofe Senior High School had 116 points. Higher Heights International School had 118 points. It was the final round—the round of death. There was one more riddle left before the end of the round. The round of death was brutal. You earned three points if you guessed a riddle correctly after the first clue. Two points after the second clue. One point after the last three clues. If you answered wrongly, you got a point deducted from your overall score. It was better not to guess at an answer if you were not sure. In the round of death the questions were thrown to both schools. The school that rang their buzzer first got the right to answer first.

I turned from Prof Kauffman and looked at the two other contestants from Sogasco who were seated by me. Both of them were seniors—Glory Agama and Innocent Kumassah. Glory was squeezing my hand so hard that I felt the bones would break. I didn't think she was breathing. Innocent was sweating so much you'd have thought someone had poured a bucket of water on him.

Across from me the three contestants of Higher Heights International School were as tense as we were. Bobby Laryea was looking straight at me.

"Contestants ready?" Prof Kaufmann asked.

All six of us nodded. My heart was pounding. The silence in the auditorium was palpable. Glory increased the pressure on my hand. Blood wasn't flowing into my fingers anymore.

"I am a univariate polynomial equation of the . . ."

BEEP. The buzzer of Higher Heights School sounded. Bobby Laryea's hand shot in the air the same moment that the last drop of blood was forced out of my fingers by the force of Glory's grip.

Bobby leaned towards the microphone and answered, "Binary form."

You could cut through the silence with a knife. All eyes were on Prof Kaufman. She shook her head. "No Bobby. A binary form is a homogeneous bivariate polynomial. Sogasco over to you."

I wondered vaguely if I'd ever use my left hand again. Glory's grip was tighter than a vice.

"Clue one: I am a univariate polynomial equation of the second degree." Prof Kaufman lifted her head to look at our table. None of us reached for the buzzer.

"Clue two: I can be written in the form 'A, X squared plus . . .'"

BUZZ. The buzzer on our table sounded. I was surprised to find my hand resting on it. Both Glory and Innocent were looking at me. Glory had officially murdered all five of my fingers.

"Yes, Yayra?" Prof Kaufmann said.

I froze. In my mind's eye I could see what Prof Kaufmann had been about to say: $ax^2+bx+c=0$. I could see it as clear as daylight. The only problem was I had forgotten what it was called.

"Yayra?" Prof Kaufmann prompted.

Opposite me all three contestants of Higher Heights International School glared at me. I shut my eyes and tried hard to remember.

"Sogasco, you know the rules. Failure to answer attracts the same penalty as a wrong answer."

I opened my eyes just in time to see the three contestants of Higher Heights sit up straighter. Hope was burning in their eyes. Bobby was trying unsuccessfully to hide a smile. I turned to Prof Kaufmann and said, "A quadratic equation."

The hall erupted when Prof Kaufmann smiled. No one heard her say, "Correct." Students and staff of Sogasco were on their feet. They were hollering, pumping their fists, clapping and screaming. I wondered if they'd all get punished for failing to 'conduct themselves in an orderly manner, both within the campus and elsewhere'.

"Glory, you can let go of my hand now," I said. She did and hugged me so hard that I knew for sure she had broken one of my ribs. I waved to Mama, Uncle Larweh, Auntie Cee, Miss Naa, Mr Budu-Smith and DJ Samsizzle. It wasn't just the entire school that had shown up for the finals; almost the entire Sogakofe town had come to support us. Even a delegation from the chief's palace, led by the queenmother, was here. Dede and Sofi were the only ones in blue uniforms who had broad smiles on their faces.

As Prof Kaufmann declared Sogakofe Senior High School winners of the National Maths and Science Quiz, our choir and students started singing our anthem. Allison was all over the place taking pictures for the school newspaper. Glory, Innocent and I were presented with the trophy. Newsmen were busy either taking pictures or filming the event. We walked down the stage and presented the trophy to Mari Jata, who was in another 'hovering' skirt suit. This one was green with white pinstripes, the school colours. She was smiling so much that I knew her smiling muscles would hurt afterwards. She had not used them in such a long time; I was surprised they even remembered how to make a smile. She hugged each one of us in turn and said, '*Ayekoo*'. We got passed from one group of huggers to another. When it was Gbabladza's turn he said, "So that's where I know you from! I saw you on TV two years ago."

"Hey, Losty," Nana Ama Attakyia called from behind me.

"My name is Yayra. It means blessing."

"Yayra, you force *paa*," she said with respect in her eyes.

The contestants from Higher Heights came over to congratulate us. Afterwards Bobby lingered to talk. "Congratulations," he said.

"Thanks," I said, as I scanned the crowd looking for a face.

"I've been meaning to ask, if you'd like . . . if maybe you'd like us to get back together."

I smiled. A smile tugged at the corner of Bobby's lips. His

face brightened and then he noticed I was looking over his shoulder.

"I'm already going out with someone," I said.

I walked away from him and into Jamal's waiting arms. "You did it," he said hugging me really tight. I didn't worry about my ribs breaking. I was enjoying the thousand electric sensations flowing through my body.

"We did, didn't we? I was so scared."

"I'm not talking about the quiz. I always knew you'd win that."

He took my hand as we headed to the school bus and laughed when he saw I had no idea what he was talking about.

"You made Mari Jata smile.

GLOSSARY

aboloo	– meal made from steamed corn dough
akple	– an Ewe meal made from cooking fermented maize flour and cassava flour. It is usually accompanied with soup, stew or pepper
aponkye nkrakra	– goat meat light soup
atakpame	– houses built with mud bricks
atsiagbekor	– traditional war dance of the Ewes
ayekoo	– well done / congratulations
bofrot	– fried balls of dough. Similar to doughnuts
banku	– meal made from cooking corn and cassava dough
chofi	– fried turkey tail
fetri detsi	– Ewe for okra soup
fufu	– meal made by pounding boiled plantain and cassava
hɔme	– Ewe for room

jollof	– dish made from boiling rice in meat or fish stew
langa- langa	– scythe-like type of weeding instrument with a thin metal blade
mami wata/ papa wata	– mermaid/ merman
medekuku	– Ewe for please
mia woezor loo	– Ewe for you're welcome
ntosuɔɔ	– Twi for a bonus item given after a purchase
okada	– commercial motorcycle
Saloon mango	– This type of mango was originally brought into Ghana from Sierra Leone and was corrupted to Sa'Leone mango and finally to what it's commonly called now, saloon mango.
shitɔ	– hot spicy pepper sauce
too known	– conceited
trotro	– commercial bus
waakye	– dish of boiled rice and beans. Eaten with salad, *gari*, spaghetti and fish or meat stew
wee	– marijuana
wele	– cooked cow hide

Printed at Tan Prints